MW00654881

1-800-IRELAND

A Sweet Contemporary Romance

JOSIE RIVIERA

INTRODUCTION

To keep up on newly released ebooks, paperbacks, Large Print Paperbacks, audiobooks, as well as exclusive sales, sign up for Josie's Newsletter today.

As a thank you, I'll send you a Free PDF ... The Beauty Of ...

Josie's Newsletter

Did you know that according to a Yale University study, people who read books live longer?

This book is dedicated to all my wonderful readers who have supported me every inch of the way.
THANK YOU!

PRAISE AND AWARDS

USA TODAY bestselling author

CHAPTER ONE

Why did I decide to do this? I must've been madder than a box of frogs.

Kathleen Kelly nodded politely while listening to Candee, her Realtor, although she scarcely paid attention. While she tried to come up with an animated reply, her mind spun. She hoped she hadn't made the biggest mistake of her life.

I'm in America. I've done it.

Meanwhile, Candee gushed on and on about Roses, their picture-perfect North Carolina town. Voted one of the best places to live by a national magazine, Roses frequently persuaded travelers passing through to sell their homes and relocate there.

Kathleen grinned, because she was one of those travelers. However, she hadn't passed through Roses. Her Dublin hometown was 3600 miles away.

The internet was a marvelous thing, connecting people from all around the world. Finally, after months of preparation, her dream of owning a business had become a reality.

Cause for celebration?

In truth, she'd been full of starry-eyed dreams and didn't

know what to expect—this being America with its laid-back style. However, she'd found that professionalism and punctuality were respected here, judging by how efficiently Candee had handled the real estate closing.

She eyed the run-down exterior, the broken-down wooden front door that looked like it had once been painted turquoise. Moss flourished beneath the eaves, and numerous shingles were missing. The brick façade was crumbling in several places.

This wasn't Betty's Diner anymore. From here on in, this was her place: Kathleen's Teahouse.

Critically, she assessed her reflection in the smudged plate-glass front window. She'd swept her red-gold hair up at the crown, and pinned the overly long ends back from her face. Tired lines etched the corners of her dark eyes, and the blush of color she'd applied along her cheekbones had disappeared, leaving her complexion pale. Her lips, which she'd always deemed too full, looked a tad solemn.

Despite the sunny day, she'd dressed in a suede skirt, thick black tights and ankle boots.

Budding leaves on the tulip magnolia trees whispered of spring, and buttery-yellow daffodils had begun to open. So different from Ireland, where hawthorn hedges wouldn't bloom until May.

"So, what do you think of your new business on Pine Cone Lane?" Candee asked.

"Everything is brilliant, absolutely brilliant," Kathleen lied effectively. Sometimes white lies were best to hide her reservations because the place wasn't nearly as brilliant as all that.

In its heyday, the former greasy-spoon diner had served countless meals, the floors and countertops spic and span. However, it had been boarded up in recent months, which was why she'd snagged the place at a steal before the building went into foreclosure.

With a silent groan, she estimated the number of weeks it would take to sand and repaint, outfit the kitchen and hire staff, and the numerous unexpected details that would surface.

She came up with months, not weeks, although she reassured herself there was no point in olagonin'—whining and complaining—because it only made things more difficult.

However, since she'd arrived in America, being anxious had become her forte.

The long weeks of anticipation and tension had taken their toll and kept her awake at night, and she could think of nothing she'd like better than a tub soak with the lavender soap she'd brought from Ireland. Followed by a lengthy, leisurely nap.

Resignedly, she knew a nap would be out of the question for a long time.

Perhaps forever.

She paused to stand back, surveying the building. If she thought objectively rather than with her emotions, she understood that she wouldn't be able to accomplish everything by herself, especially within a five-week timeline.

She'd scheduled her grand opening on St. Patrick's Day, deeming the date fitting and appropriate.

She envisioned painting the shingles a serene shade of soft-green, overstated by a burgundy-striped canvas awning, much like the awning gracing The Ground Café, her former employer's coffee shop in Dublin. And she wanted outdoor seating on the patio, allowing customers to dine at wrought iron tables beneath vintage-style Edison light bulbs.

Curb appeal. That's what the place needed.

She focused on which project she would dive into first—the interior or the exterior.

She was weighing the pros and cons when Candee asked,

"You're not having second thoughts about moving to America, are you? I realize it's a huge undertaking."

"Of course not," Kathleen said. "Ireland was getting a little too small for me."

At thirty-five years old, her mantra had become *pursue my dreams or bust*. Besides, it was too late to check out, things being what they were. Her former coworkers knew she was embarking on a refreshingly different chapter in her life, and it would be disheartening to admit defeat.

Kathleen fidgeted with the gold watch on her wrist, a going-away gift from her employer, Danny Brady.

"Also," she continued, "baking and the restaurant trade are second nature to me. I've spent half my life managing a coffee shop."

Candee covered Kathleen's hand. "Sometimes a fresh start is as simple as buying a dilapidated building and getting on an airplane."

"Did I say that?"

"Oh, and much more, because you not only said it, you did it," Candee said. "You've created your dream life."

Kathleen shook her head. "I used to be smart and sensible."

"In the present circumstances, you're even smarter," Candee said. "And you're strong and beautiful. The first time we Skyped, I couldn't get over how put together you were. You'd already composed a business plan."

Kathleen offered a brittle smile. "Don't believe everything on your computer screen."

"Positive thinking, plus action, leads to accomplishment. You're a doer."

"Despite what my so-called friends advised," Kathleen replied.

"Weren't they supportive?"

"Aye, in a polite sort of way. They gave me rock-hard,

unsolicited advice." For some reason, her thoughts kept darting back to Ireland, and a sense of isolation rolled through her. "They wanted to protect me from making a mistake."

She longed to tell someone about the successful closing of her new property, the deep-blue sky gracing the warm Carolina days, the way the sweetgum tree branches swayed in the pleasant morning breezes.

But there was no one to tell. Danny and his wife, Clara, were busy with their own lives, with a wee one on the way.

"You'll love Roses, and I predict your teahouse will become a tea emporium," Candee said.

"What in the world is that?"

"An emporium is a retail store selling a variety of goods."

"I plan to serve food—Irish tea and scones, sandwiches and cakes. I'm not a chain of fancy shops."

"Well, you should be. Also sell tea and teapots, because you and Roses are poised for success. I can feel it."

Kathleen smiled. Aye, Roses was enchanting. The once sleepy town was thriving, and the lush green grass packed neatly between the brick sidewalks reminded her a wee bit of Ireland.

Except that it wasn't ...

Remembrances of lyrical brogues brought a poignant yearning to Kathleen's chest that stopped her cold. She hadn't realized she'd be so homesick. With her accent, she'd already found that oftentimes her words got misheard and misunderstood, and she'd had a hard time communicating even though everyone spoke the same language—English.

"This area will get a lot of foot traffic, especially on warm spring and summer evenings," Candee said. "Here in the Carolinas we enjoy a temperate climate, so don't rule out winter or fall, either."

"Unlike Ireland." Kathleen chuckled.

"Does it truly rain buckets?"

"Our term is bucketing down," Kathleen said, repeating the standard Irish joke. "Although the rain is at least warm in the summer."

Candee laughed. "Is it windy?"

"Not much." Kathleen lifted her shoulders in a teasing shrug. "Except small children and pets are sometimes blown clear away to England."

"Believe me, you'll enjoy the weather here," Candee concluded with a laugh. Gently, she urged Kathleen to the diner's doorway.

Kathleen blinked at the dazzling noon sunlight and realized her stomach was growling. She hadn't eaten anything except a slice of her homemade Irish brown bread when she'd woken at six a.m.

"What do you think of your upstairs apartment?" Candee asked. "Internet photos don't do a place justice, but housing above your teahouse is a money saver. You won't have to pay rent nor commute."

"Aye. Although truth be told, it's all in a little worse shape than I expected."

"Manageable, though, I trust?" Candee's puzzled frown swung from the door to Kathleen. "I realize it needs curtains."

"It lacks a lot more than updated curtains," Kathleen said with a laugh. "And it will take an army of crewmen to get everything in working order by St. Patrick's Day."

"My husband, Teddy, is a contractor. He'll get the place turned around for you in no time." Candee shook back a strand of red hair that had come loose from her braid, exposing a pair of gold cross earrings, the only jewelry she wore except for her wedding rings. Even without an ounce of makeup, the woman was stunning, her green eyes gleaming whenever she discussed her husband and their adopted son, Joseph.

In addition to being a Realtor, Candee had opened an afterschool daycare facility in her home for disadvantaged children in the community. On several occasions, Kathleen wondered how Candee was able to do it all. She'd been inspired to match her stamina and ambition.

"As long as there's running water, a kitchen and a bathroom in my apartment," Kathleen said, "my needs are met."

"Good. Your reference from Danny Brady was excellent, by the way."

"I never missed a day of work."

"And he said your brown bread flew off the shelves whenever it was featured."

"He granted me the option to take my recipe to America, and I ran with it."

"Free and clear?"

"Danny understood I was drained. After countless years as his head assistant, I wanted a change." Kathleen wished the warmth burning her cheeks didn't give her away. Why couldn't she compartmentalize her second thoughts like she did everything else in her life?

Because she was excited.

And mildly terrified.

"I expect he and his wife will come to America and visit me someday," she finished.

Candee studied her. "So, at present, you're alone."

"Aye." Kathleen considered saying more, to explain she always felt lonely despite her attempts to build relationships.

She kept her lips sealed. Some words were better left unsaid.

In a little over two years, she'd been duped by a man not once, but twice. First, by a moneyed Italian she'd met on the internet who had turned out to be, surprise, surprise, a young boy. And then, Alexander, an American businessman, had played her for a muppet—a fool.

Danny Brady and his bodyguard, Ian, had said Alexander was too talkative. Talkative? Hah! What an understatement! Charmer was more like it, and Alexander was so smooth-talking he could sell ya an eye out of your own head. He'd had her believing he was genuinely interested in her. When she'd fallen for him, his charisma had changed to controlling. He'd quickly become domineering and expected her to be subservient.

As Candee continued to study her, Kathleen offered, "The man I believed I loved was actually two different men. He was fine as long as things went his way and I was passive." She shrugged and tried to act unconcerned. "Although being submissive isn't in my nature. As I advanced in my career, our relationship quickly fell apart."

"You said you wanted a fresh start, and you've created it. Here's to new men and extraordinary opportunities." Candee gestured to the doorway.

"I'll take the opportunities minus the men," Kathleen said. Truly, she was done with con men, eejits—idiots—who expected women to take a back seat to them and their opinions. Men who exuded personality while keeping a close watch on their own agendas. Men who fired off derisive comments for no other reason than to feel superior.

She was a woman who had helped Danny Brady's Ground Café achieve fame. Here and now, with determination and hard work, she'd make her teahouse a noteworthy addition to this quaint little town.

"During our Skype sessions, I mentioned that your teahouse will offset Keiran O'Malley's Irish pub nicely." Candee pointed to a side street. "His building isn't far from here."

"Keiran's cousin, William, first spoke of Roses and recommended you as a Realtor, which is why I messaged you," Kathleen said. "Fortunately, I zoomed in on this town fairly quickly."

"William lives in Dublin, right?"

"He also knows Sean, my coworker from The Ground Café. Both men wanted to date me, and I turned Sean down flat."

"And William?"

"He frequented the café a couple times a week. We dated for a short while after my breakup with Alexander until I realized I wasn't ready for a romantic involvement." Kathleen swallowed, giving herself a breather before continuing. "Sean still texts me now and then. He wishes to come to America to help me with my new business."

"Is that a good thing or a bad thing?"

"I'm not certain. Sean is competent, but I can't imagine he'd actually fancy working for me. He and I were on the same level as managers." She exhaled. "At any rate, William had told me that Keiran loves it in Roses."

"He's married to my sister, Desiree. They are extremely happy."

"I've heard."

Happy. Such an elusive term.

"Keiran said that life called him back to Roses. Maybe the town called you here too."

Kathleen reflected on Candee's words. She'd read about life's calling in self-help books and tuned in to endless podcasts on the subject. Sometimes, it seemed like she'd waited her entire life for a voice to explain which bend in the road led to happiness.

Nevertheless, if one's calling was a voice whispering in her ear, she hadn't heard a sound. Perhaps a calling was the Lord tapping her on the shoulder. Either way, she'd known in her gut that Roses was the ideal spot, and everything had clicked into place.

"In any case, here I am," she replied.

Candee opened her arms, firmly clasping them around Kathleen. "And this is the dawn of the grandest adventure of your life."

Tears welled in Kathleen's eyes—a mix of joy, fear, and reservations. She'd chosen her destiny, following in the footprints of the Irish immigrant.

Don't be an eejit, her inner voice chided. *You're launching a teahouse, not fleeing from a potato famine.*

"And I can't wait to introduce you to everyone," Candee said. "Desiree and Keiran, my husband Teddy, and our son, Joseph—"

"Aye. When the time comes." Now she was sounding standoffish.

She drew a see-through container from her leather shoulder bag. "Before I forget, I baked a loaf of my brown bread for you this morning."

Candee stepped back. "You haven't been here two days and you're already baking bread in your apartment?"

"I ran the oven before I even unpacked." She handed the container to Candee. "This is a thank-you gift for taking care of the million incidentals that came with an international real-estate transaction. And, for fixing up my apartment before I arrived."

"My pleasure. Decorating is my thing, and you advised me on your likes and dislikes. In fact, you were quite decisive."

"I don't have much of a knack for it."

"Oh, but you do."

Kathleen envisioned the packing boxes strewn throughout her flat's hallway, the luggage and clothes piled by her bed. She should have put away her belongings a while ago.

Instead, she'd drawn on a ruffled apron, let a batch of dough rise, and baked.

"Take a bite," she urged.

Candee obliged, closing her eyes as she nibbled. "This bread is one of the best baked goods I've ever tasted. And that's saying a lot, because my friend in Miami owns ..."

"I plan to sell Irish brown bread every day," Kathleen said, grinning broadly at the compliment. "Although I'll need to sell more than bread."

"What about pizza?" Candee asked.

"I'll leave pizza to the pizzeria in town. Presently, I'll turn my energy into outfitting the bakery with delicious Irish desserts and an array of tea selections. In Ireland, people aren't in such a hurry. We savor every moment, and I intend to create the same experience in my teahouse."

"Unlike America," Candee said.

"Comfy couches and free Wi-Fi," Kathleen went on. "Brewed tea in a variety of flavors—chamomile, mint, and a host of exotic herbal leaves."

Her ideas overflowed. Were they too ambitious?

"Have you set your hours?" Candee stooped down at the doorway, muttering about the weather stripping not being sufficiently tight to prevent air leaks.

"I'll open at eleven, and close by nine at night."

"You realize you're describing ten-hour work days?"

"Aye." Like a shot, Kathleen's brain worked rapidly. "I'm still on the lookout for locally sourced ingredients so I can serve healthy salads, sandwiches, and wraps. For dinner, stone-baked pita bread topped with goat cheese and caramelized onions will be a nightly special."

Candee linked arms with Kathleen and walked to the side of the building, where rickety exterior stairs led to the second floor. "What you're describing is enough work for twenty people. And that pita bread sounds a lot like pizza."

"It's Irish pizza, so no competition with the local pizzeria." Deciding on her menu options, Kathleen hardly realized Candee had come to a determined stop while saying a man's name twice.

Rob. Rob.

"Who is Rob?" Kathleen asked.

"He's a dear friend and owns a string of popular bakeries." For some reason, Candee's pitch heightened. "His chain is called Rob's Marvelous Muffins and is based in the Miami area where he lives. He's delightful and funny and easy-going—"

"Brilliant, I'm sure." Kathleen went back to the menu choices in her mind. Irish bacon and poached eggs, or a traditional Irish breakfast complete with roasted tomatoes and mushrooms? Perhaps beef burgers and cider glazed salmon for lunch.

No. She reined in her thoughts. This wasn't a full-scale restaurant.

"I'll begin advertising for employees soon and start with a modest staff," she said, "Did I tell you I won't be serving alcohol?"

"Yes, and I applaud your decision."

"Thanks. I've had enough of that in Ireland. People going out on the lash and stumbling home in the wee hours." Kathleen waved a dismissive hand. "I'll leave the drinking to the pubs."

She looked back on the intervention Clara Brady had staged for her alcoholic brother, Seamus. Little good that had done. Once a person was addicted, it was often a long road to wellness.

"What are the requisite number of ovens for a bakery?" Candee asked.

"Certainly a small commercial oven, plus a full-size convection oven is necessary. Also, a deck oven for layer cakes and breads." Kathleen frowned as she considered all the equipment yet to purchase. "Where will I buy a mixer and a—"

"You'll need someone knowledgeable to advise you. Fortunately, Rob has extensive retail bakery experience. He studied at a prestigious culinary school in Florida offering lots of hands-on experience." Candee plucked her cell-phone from her purse. The excitement in her voice matched the glow in her eyes. "He was voted Miami's most successful entrepreneur, and he's just the right person to help you."

Whoever this Rob was, he'd be overwhelmed when he saw what needed to be completed in five weeks.

Unless, of course, he was a miracle worker.

CHAPTER TWO

"Rob's Marvelous Muffins." Realizing both hands were a sticky mess from rolling out pastry dough, Rob Taylor answered his cell-phone, then balanced the phone against his shoulder. His gaze landed on the commercial mixer on the counter. He switched it on to prepare twenty batches of cupcakes.

Mondays weren't usually hectic, but with Valentine's Day over and the forthcoming St. Patrick's Day holiday, baking green cupcakes galore became the blueprint of the day.

Pushing out a sharp breath, he wiped his hands on the white apron tied around his protruding waist, trying to remember how many cupcakes he'd tasted that morning. One. Well, no, at least two. Okay, three, although the third had lacked his bakery's signature Irish Cream liqueur glaze.

He eyed that same liqueur set near several pounds of unsalted butter by the commercial mixer, ticking off the items on his to-do list. Next, dozens of cupcakes needed frosting.

A diet was in order, but he'd made peace with that long ago. A man owning a half-dozen bakery shops couldn't resist the smell of mouth-watering chocolate, succulent blueberry, or tart lemon muffins. At least, *he* couldn't. And there was nothing to do except, well, keep tasting.

"Rob, are you there? Hi. It's Candee."

He grinned. "How's my favorite daughter-in-law?"

"Umm, are we all of a sudden related?"

"Your husband is like a son to me." Rob silently motioned one of the bakers to shut off the timer going off on a convection oven. "So if Teddy is my son, then you're my daughter-in-law."

"I've always loved your logic, Rob." Candee chuckled. "How's the muffin business?"

"Busy. Can't complain." He muffled the phone as an employee wearing a company hat and sporting nonslip clogs ran past looking for the espresso. The featured cupcake was a combination of flour, sugar, espresso, and that Irish Cream liqueur.

"How is everyone in Roses?" Rob asked. "Is the weather warm in the Carolinas? The temperature is in the mid-seventies here in Miami."

"We're all well. It's a pleasant, sunny day and quite typical for February. Teddy sends his love." Candee paused. "Can I ask you something?"

"Anything, my lovely daughter-in-law."

"What are your views on helping a damsel in distress?"

"Like in the original silent movies where the villain wearing a top hat ties the woman to the railroad tracks? What was that guy's name again?"

"Snidely Whiplash. And no, I mean a beautiful woman needs your help."

"Wait. Who in Roses ..." Rob stopped in the middle of his sentence. "I assume you're not referring to yourself."

"Correct."

"Okay then. Who? And why me?" He glanced at his wristwatch. The lunch-hour crowd would be flooding into the bakery soon. Mentally, he estimated the hundreds of cupcakes required to refill the soon-to-be-empty display cases.

"Because you're a professional baker," Candee said. "Plus, you're a perfect gentleman."

"I appreciate the compliments, but where are we going with this conversation?"

"Do you remember my telling you about Kathleen, an Irishwoman from Dublin? She managed The Ground Café."

"Actually, I do," Rob said. "That coffee shop chain recently opened in the States."

"At the time, Kathleen was considering relocating to Roses and starting a teahouse. Well, all that talk became a reality."

Vaguely, he recalled the discussion from a few months earlier. "Congratulations. She made it over the pond okay?"

"Yes, and she's enthusiastic and vivacious and—"

"Good. Wish her luck." He paused to bark instructions to David, a new employee plunging a rack of croissants into a roll-in oven. David had been recommended by a friend of a friend, and Rob had hired him on the spot. High employee turnover and a shortage of staff left him no choice. Too bad the kid hardly looked eighteen, his checkered trousers a size too big for his skinny body, a white torque hat overpowering his small head.

According to his application, David was twenty-something.

Either kids were looking younger, Rob mused, or he was getting older.

"Don't take shortcuts," he directed the newbie. "Check the oven temperature again."

"Yes, Mr. Rob," the newbie acknowledged with a slight bow.

"Do I look like the king of England?" Rob held up a hand, palm up. "Check the temperature, or I'll have you clear out the moat around the bakery."

David gave Rob a blank look and scurried away.

Rob eyed the liqueur. He was inclined to grab the bottle and pour himself a large glass.

Clueless. This next generation was absolutely clueless. Surely the kid realized there was no moat.

The clanging of a pan had him cupping the phone to his ear. "Sorry, Candee. I'd like to chitchat, but it's busier than I anticipated today. Can I call you back tonight? Or better yet, in April."

"Things won't be busy in April?"

"I forgot Easter is in April. Maybe May."

"Isn't Mother's Day in May?"

"June. We'll say June." He ran an irritated hand over his bald head and sighed. "June is the month for weddings. Apparently, a baker's job is never done."

"Coincidentally, Rob, she's a baker too."

"Who?"

"Kathleen. The Irishwoman."

"Right. As we've established, so am I. Tell her cheers, or whatever those Irish people say, and to prepare to never sleep."

"She's lovely."

"Bravo."

"She baked me an Irish brown bread," Candee said. "Her special recipe, and it's delicious."

He slanted over the table to snap off the electric mixer before the over-mixed batter resulted in dense, gummy cupcakes.

"How delicious?" He tried to decide whether he should put the phone on speaker so that he could spoon the batter into tins, or grow a third hand.

"How delicious compared to your cupcakes?" Candee asked.

"Yeah."

"Her bread is the best baked good this side of the Atlantic."

Whoa. Compared to his award-winning cupcakes? Rob frowned and held out a hand to stop an employee from rushing over to him.

"Hold on," he said to Candee. He laid his phone on the counter, yanked off his apron, and stalked to a quiet spot by a window. "Okay, I'm back."

"She is overwhelmed," Candee said. "Relocating to a different country, launching a business from scratch ... I can't imagine how she'll accomplish everything. Do you recall the broken-down diner on Pine Cone Lane? It's been unoccupied for a while."

"The diner is located not far from Keiran's pub, right?"

At his mention of Keiran, Rob rubbed a hand over his eyes. Perhaps he should tell Candee how guilty he felt that he'd been unable to attend the grand re-opening of O'Malley's, the pub Keiran had inherited from his father. Although Keiran and his wife, Desiree, had assured Rob they understood he couldn't leave Miami during the middle of an extensive baking exhibition, he'd missed being in Roses to support them.

"Good memory, Rob," Candee said. "And Kathleen intends to create an old-world teahouse. The problem is the place is screaming for a total remodel. She's experienced, but—"

"What can I do?" Rob conjured up the image of a cherubic, delicate Irishwoman. Slight and fragile, with flaming-red hair and freckles, staring wide-eyed at an undertaking far too large for her.

"You have the expertise and bakery know-how," Candee said.

"Does she need capital and an investor?" Understanding that all new restaurants were under-capitalized, Rob automatically reached for his wallet. A foolish move, he realized, unless cash flew through the phone lines. And even more foolish because he wouldn't see a return on his investment for three to four years.

"She needs advice and support," Candee said. "She's laser-focused on a St. Patrick's Day opening."

"Does she have a business license and sales permit?"

"All set. Fortunately, the diner was already permitted as a restaurant."

"Health and fire department permits?"

"Done."

"Is she making alterations to the building?"

"Major." For the first time, Candee hesitated. "Why?"

He peered out the window. The wrought-iron tables facing his bakery were filled with customers. Between the palm tree border outlining the seating area, low-flowering crepe myrtle trees added pops of vibrant pink blossoms. The effect created a natural arbor, and shade from the bright Florida sun. If customers were comfortable, they tended to stay longer and buy more baked goods.

"She'll need a building permit and possibly a parking permit," he said.

"Good point. I'll check into it."

"Does her business have a name?"

"Kathleen's Teahouse, and the sign is being designed as we speak. She's keeping true to the logo of the old diner. And she's planning to be open ten hours a day and serve breakfast, light lunches, and dinner, as well as tea and baked goods."

"She should add five hours to the beginning and end of her shift for preparation and clean-up," he said. "Tell her to hire a lot of help, which is forever challenging. Bakery employees find the labor exhausting—both mentally and physically."

"Because of those hot ovens, and they're on their feet so much," Candee commiserated. "Anyway, it's my long-winded way of asking you to come to Roses and give her a hand."

He delayed his response, preparing to launch into a thousand reasons why he couldn't leave his bakeries at such a chaotic time.

"Rob," Candee said, "I know how busy you are."

"You read my mind."

"And I wouldn't phone you if she wasn't in such a bind. The woman is beyond desperate and the place is bleeding money."

Frowning, he strode to the counter and took a sip of the liqueur directly from the bottle. There were plenty of other bottles in the storage room, he rationalized.

"She can email me. No charge for free advice," he said.

Silence on the other end of the phone. Oops. Maybe he'd sounded a little too harsh. A second glance at his watch revealed half past noon. The bakery would be overflowing with people.

He pondered. He hadn't been able to attend the opening of Keiran's pub. However, if he booked a quick trip to Roses, he could be back in Miami by Tuesday.

His bakeries were all closed on Sunday. He'd made the decision since going back to church. It was a religious choice, and a way to honor God.

"You can stay with me and Teddy," Candee pressed. "It will give you an opportunity to see Joseph, the beagles, and Joseph's horse."

The trip made perfect sense. He'd visit with everyone, plus extend his expertise to the Irishwoman. Furthermore, Roses was absolutely delightful in its slow-paced, countrified way. It would be good to get out of Miami's rat race for three days. Lately, he'd felt exhausted both emotionally and physically.

"Maybe you're right," he murmured.

"Fabulous," Candee said. "You'll love Kathleen. She's all Irish wit and charm. Trust me, you'll want to listen to her brogue all day."

For some reason, Rob felt a little toss of excitement.

Why?

This trip was about a hurried getaway, not meeting an Irishwoman with milky-white skin who brewed perfect cups of tea. She couldn't possibly deal with all that owning a bakery, teahouse, and full-fledged restaurant entailed, so he'd set her straight.

If she was the determined type, she'd remain in Roses, although it was more likely she'd high-tail it back to Ireland before the end of March.

"So when did you say you were arriving?" Candee asked.

"Can Teddy pick me up at the Asheville airport?"

"Absolutely."

Rob took another swig of liqueur. "I'll fly out early Sunday morning, because Saturday is a high-volume day. I'll attend church services on Saturday evening here in Miami."

"Hurray," Candee said with a joyous laugh. "We'll do the same. See you soon."

He started to say more, then stopped, bidding goodbye and clicking off the phone.

How had he been talked into something so quickly?

Truth be told, he was intrigued. This Irishwoman displayed grit by leaving everything behind and coming to America. He guessed she was probably homesick.

He braced a hand on the window sill and stared at the roll-in oven, where smoke was emerging.

"Mr. Rob, do you think the croissants are finished baking?" David, the newbie, asked.

"Did you set the timer?"

"No." David rummaged through a stack of boxes near the oven. "Where is it?

"Do you smell smoke?"

"A little."

"I'd say the entire batch is burned." Rob handed the newbie two oven mitts and snapped a string of instructions. The young man paled and promptly complied, apologizing because it was all his fault.

Rob agreed.

Mitts at the ready, David opened the oven door to a large quantity of burned croissants. He cursed, then swung around. "Are you going to fire me on my first day, Mr. Rob?"

"For cursing?"

"Because ... because the croissants are burned."

"I'll give you another chance because I like you."

With that, Rob pushed open the adjoining door to his bustling bakery. Fortunately, no one realized that under his gruff exterior, he was really a marshmallow.

CHAPTER THREE

The following Sunday, Rob stepped off the plane at the modern Asheville airport. He and Teddy exchanged greetings with a clap on the back.

Now that he'd arrived, Rob checked his phone for messages. Although his bakeries weren't open, he oversaw a skeleton crew as they prepared products and ingredients for Monday.

Freeze the stock we selected before you punch out, Rob texted his associate manager.

Roger, his manager replied.

Roger? Really? Who says that? Wasn't the term used for radio communication?

Teddy chuckled, eyeing Rob's exasperated sigh. "I don't miss those days."

"Of slaving over a hot oven? I wish I could say neither do I, but I'm still baking after all these years. Sometimes I wonder if I should sell everything and move to Hawaii."

"Or the Carolinas," Teddy suggested.

"You're always trying to convince me to relocate here."

"I'm simply fulfilling my role as your best friend, and

friends like to be near each other. For camaraderie. And support."

The men had been chums for years. A decade earlier, they'd met at a men's cooking class. Rob had discovered he loved baking and pursued a culinary arts degree. Upon graduation, he'd opened a prosperous bakery chain. Teddy decided he didn't want to be in charge of all that dough (he'd quoted the pun from Julia Child), and, with Rob's capital, became a real estate professional and flipped homes.

After Rob retrieved his luggage, he and Teddy settled into Teddy's pickup truck. Morning sun lightened the sky, and the beauty of North Carolina—from the majestic waterfalls to an old-fashioned swimming hole—brought a sense of relaxation.

"Beautiful state, isn't it? Candee and I love it here," Teddy said.

"Yeah. I may rent a car for an afternoon trip tomorrow."

"You won't be able to explore everything in a few hours, so file it under your list of reasons to move here."

"I don't have a list of reasons," Rob said.

"You should." A grin flashed across Teddy's features. "The other day, Candee read a travel brochure advertising outdoor dining by a pool of water in Asheville. She also cited many art galleries tucked away in little towns within an hour's car ride of Roses."

"Sightseeing it is, then."

"I'd go with you, but I'm tied up with renovating the teahouse, plus helping Candee with her daycare facility. And, needless to say, seeing to Joseph. I assume you'll go by yourself?" Teddy asked.

"Who else?" Rob laughed gruffly. "I can't remember when I last toured anywhere with a companion." He drew down the mirrored sun visor for a quick glance at his reflection, keenly studying the lines of fatigue around his mouth. He was closing in on fifty years old, and the strained creases were showing.

"Frankly, you seem like you need an extended vacation, my friend."

"Uh-huh. Thanks for the advice." Rob flipped up the visor, then smoothed the wrinkles on his Rob's Marvelous Muffins T-shirt. He'd worn the shirt under a navy sport jacket paired with khaki pants. A white cotton square handkerchief showed from his breast jacket pocket.

"I thought my age looked good on me, although I don't see as well as I used to." He chuckled. "Get it?"

Teddy grinned. "I can always count on you for the one-liners. I'm glad you're here. I wish you looked more rested."

Dismissing his fatigue with a wave, Rob replied to a sequence of text messages.

Teddy flicked on the blinker and merged onto the road leading to Roses. "Mind if I ask you a question?"

"Not at all," Rob replied, still absorbed in his text messaging. "I'm perfectly willing to listen. I won't guarantee an answer, though."

"When have you ever actually relaxed?"

Not in forever. Rob didn't share that fact with Teddy, as he'd probably encourage Rob to extend his stay. Although he might be tempted, his bakeries could never operate without him.

"It's high time you enjoyed life," Teddy said. "Worrying about every minute decision will only magnify your problems."

Rob paused, reflecting how best to answer. He switched on the radio to the Bee Gees singing "How Deep Is Your Love".

"Since when have you become so philosophical?" Rob asked.

"A wonderful woman changes a man." Lightly, Teddy

tapped the beat of the song on the steering wheel. "Makes him stop and think about what's truly important."

A ping on his cell-phone drew Rob's attention. His manager asked whether to close an hour later in order to customize a cake for a last-minute wedding.

If you need extra time to get the job done, then sure, Rob texted.

You'll be paying the staff overtime, the manager reminded.

What else is new? With that, Rob snapped his phone shut and jammed it into his pocket. He felt his blood pressure rising. A visit with his physician had confirmed that blood pressure medication would soon be a part of Rob's future. For the time being, he'd refused the brigade of medicines his doctor was all too willing to prescribe.

"That nice-looking Irishwoman might make the ideal companion on your sightseeing excursion," Teddy said. "She hasn't explored the area yet, either."

"Not interested. You and Keiran married the last two good women on the planet."

"There's more than two good women in the world, Rob. And a third is waiting for you to sweep her off her feet."

"Based on the number of my failed dates, a successful match for me is probably somewhere on a remote island in the Pacific. And because I'm not vacationing in the Pacific islands anytime soon, I'd say my dating days are over."

"I don't believe that for a minute." Teddy's expression puckered into a pensive frown, and Rob was reminded of Teddy's older brother, Christian, who had died in a horrific car accident. Teddy had stepped in and gained legal custody of his young nephew, Joseph.

Like his brother, Teddy was dark-eyed and tall, and Rob knew Teddy mourned the loss of his brother every day. Teddy and Candee were exemplary parents, raising a child who had been left frail and devastated after the accident. Fortunately, hours of physical therapy and boundless love had enabled the boy to rebound triumphantly.

"No wonder we never got along," Rob teased. "You're an eternal optimist."

They flew across a bridge, and crushed gravel crackled beneath the truck's tires.

"You'll find your special woman when you least expect it," Teddy said.

Really? Who? He was older now, bald, twenty pounds overweight, and set in his ways. Anyway, bachelor life suited him.

He shifted in his seat. All those long nights in his deluxe Florida condo with a sweeping view of Miami beach had passed in solitude. He filled the void with work, because loneliness only crept up when he had time to think.

He dragged his contemplations away from self-absorption, preferring to stare out the window at the picturesque landscape with a magnificent Blue Ridge mountain backdrop. They traveled past an ancient church, fields of wildflowers, and a garden of violet irises beginning to bloom.

"Candee is preparing a special brunch for us," Teddy said. "Or rather, Keiran is cooking. Desiree hasn't purchased a dining room set yet, so everyone is assembling at my house."

Keiran had met Desiree when he'd been hired to fix up Desiree's Victorian home. They'd married a few months afterward and lived a couple doors down from Candee and Teddy.

"Sounds perfect," Rob said. "I'm always up for a delicious meal."

"Be prepared for pandemonium. Our beagle, Kisses, is full grown. Plus, Candee gifted Keiran and Desiree a pup, and the dog goes everywhere with them."

"The more commotion, the better." Rob slanted his head back, viewing a row of shuttered buildings. "What town are we in?"

"We're going through Hollan Farms. It's several towns over from Roses."

"Interesting little place." Rob noted mediocre shops and an enormous hotel that dominated the main street. "Someone should give it some TLC. Does anyone live here?"

"At last count there were a few inhabitants. A major factory moved out a while ago, leaving a proverbial ghost town. I heard the entire town is for sale, and the asking price is several million dollars."

Not bad for a place with lots of potential, Rob mused. He was, after all, a businessperson.

A businessperson who could barely handle a half-dozen bakeries in Miami, let alone an entire town.

As they passed through, Teddy indicated the rotted wood on a boarded-up ice cream parlor, then focused a conspiratorial smile on Rob. "Don't even speculate about buying this town to renovate. You have enough on your hands, and should be slowing down to enjoy your wealth."

Rob chuckled. His friend was a mind-reader and knew him like the back of his hand.

"I have absolutely no intention of buying anything," Rob defended brusquely. When skeptical amusement crossed Teddy's face, Rob immediately changed the subject. "How is Keiran's pub?"

"The first few weeks were hectic. At present he's settled in and doing what he loves. Desiree took an extended leave from her law firm to hostess at the pub."

As they entered Roses, Teddy stopped at a crossroads and rounded toward Thompson Lane. The street was lined with trees, large older homes, and plenty of acreage. Window boxes overflowed with velvety purple pansies, ferns, and tulip bulbs, staying true to the traditional origins of the town. Teddy pointed out Keiran and Desiree's Victorian as they drove by.

"Ready to meet Kathleen after brunch?" Teddy eased his truck around the circular driveway and parked in front of his three-story house with its octagonal tower and multi-gabled roof. "Candee has immersed herself in Kathleen's business and vows to make it as popular as Keiran's pub. Too bad the place isn't open yet. Imagine when it is."

"All this Irish charm in one pint-size town," Rob mused. "Sure, I planned on meeting her."

"Excellent." Teddy grinned. "Because she's expecting you."

That afternoon, Kathleen stood on her front stoop and watched a well-dressed bald man wearing a navy sport jacket and khaki pants emerge from Teddy's truck.

Her heart thudded with nervousness. The past few days, endless work had muddled the hours. Today she'd been awake before dawn, baking, attending church, and revising her business plan. She made a mental note to ask Candee if there were any local social media sites where she could advertise.

She'd heard so many stories about the legendary Rob and his marvelous muffins that anticipating his arrival had become an exercise in self-discipline. She flattened the collar of her checkered blouse, critically reviewing her navy-print slacks and sensible leather flats. The mint-green cardigan over her shoulders warded off the midafternoon chill.

She'd half-expected Rob to wear a chef jacket and black trousers, while brandishing a wooden mixing spoon. However, the man confidently striding toward her was solid and broad-shouldered, a warm smile crinkling his face and accentuating his electric-blue eyes. Instead of a wooden spoon, he carried a reflective silver wine bag.

"So you're the lovely Irish rose." He came to the doorstep, stopped within a foot of her, and beamed.

"And you're the famous Rob, who owns bakeries all over Florida."

"Only a half dozen, and they're all located in the Miami area." He grinned. "It saves me from driving all across the state."

"Well, I'll leave you two to get acquainted," Teddy called from his truck. "Rob, when you want a lift back to my place, text me."

"Thanks. Probably in a couple hours." Rob's wave to Teddy was quick before he veered to her. "However, I confess I'm at an impasse."

"A confession already? We just met."

"And an impasse."

She lifted an eyebrow. "Impasse?

"Yes, because I may never want to leave." He extended his hand. "I'm Rob."

"I gathered. Why are you staring at me, Rob?"

"Because you're beautiful, and not at all who I expected."

Near the curb, she heard the purring of Teddy's truck engine.

"Who did you expect?" she asked.

"Not someone who makes me flustered because she's so gorgeous. I get tongue-tied around women like you."

"What?"

"Tongue-tied. At a loss for words."

"For a tongue-tied guy, you're speaking quite well, although I appreciate the compliment." She forced herself to stop and think. "*Was* that a compliment?"

"Absolutely. You remind me of Maureen O'Hara from *Miracle on 34th Street*."

"I love that film. Maureen was originally from Dublin and only twenty-seven years old when she played the role," Kathleen said.

She felt Teddy's gaze on them for another moment before the engine roared and he pulled away from the curb.

"I'm Kathleen, by the way." She accepted Rob's hand. Large and firm, he had the hands of a construction worker with calluses along the base of his fingers. From hours using a rolling pin, she surmised, because she had the same.

"The beautiful Kathleen." He gave a smile, and her heart skipped a beat.

She regarded him, trying to gauge if his words were sincere. She might have given a flippant response, the cool disinterest she employed whenever she suspected men were coming on to her. But wait. Was he—

No, certainly not. Aside from the age difference, he was accomplished and well-educated. She was a country girl who'd grown up in County Galway before moving to Dublin.

He let go of her hand, tugged a bottle out of the bag, and offered it to her. "This is for you. Do you drink Irish liqueur?"

"Tea. I drink tea." She examined the label. "Imported from Ireland?"

"Yes, although this bottle is from Miami. Consider it a housewarming gift. It's a little reminder of your country in case you were homesick."

How did he know she was homesick? A ripple of sadness brought a sting of tears to her eyes that she quickly blinked away.

His gaze fastened on her. "I use the liqueur as an ingredient for a cupcake glaze."

"Thanks."

"I like it," he said.

"Liqueur? Oh, I'm sure." She stuck the bottle in the bag and set it on the stoop. "Most Irish men love a drink or two." *Or three or four.*

"On special occasions?" Rob asked.

"On any occasion. Many were on the lash."

"Meaning?"

"Irish slang for going out drinking." Ruefully, she laughed. "I've learned to stick with tea, though."

"In that case, so will I." That beam again, flashing charisma, and firing an attraction inside her that took her utterly by surprise.

"And I'll teach you how to create the best buttery glaze on the East Coast," he said.

When, exactly? Candee had told Kathleen that Rob was only in town until Tuesday. He was a wealthy, successful man, setting aside a few days from his busy calendar. Most likely he was overconfident, a tad entitled, and considered his time more valuable than anyone else's.

"Like you, I'm also pressed for any spare hour these days," she said.

"Oh. Sure." He kept his beam. "I understand."

The appeal of his handsome face caused her pulse to leap, and an awkward heartbeat went by. He waited, apparently, for her to elaborate about the host of things she had yet to do.

She didn't respond, just stared at him as if she'd never seen a man before. She should invite him up to her apartment for tea. However, while she was usually neat as a pin, the living room and bedroom were in dusty disarray and boxes were everywhere.

"However, we have a dilemma," he continued.

So do I, she thought. Aloud, she asked, "Which is?"

"How will I prove who is the better baker if we don't bake together?"

There it was. A not-so-silent gauntlet thrown down between two professional chefs.

Or did he propose more than a bake-off contest?

"We're together now," she pointed out.

"We're not baking. I can show you my cupcake recipe, the one crying out for my celebrated buttery glaze. I presume you store flour and sugar in your apartment's pantry?"

"Of course. I raced to the corner grocer as soon as I arrived in Roses."

"Good." He brought levity to the moment with another smile. "I've heard your Irish brown bread is fabulous."

Aye, they could bake, but she preferred to chat. Here, on her front porch, sitting on the two white wicker rocking chairs Candee had restored, enjoying a cheery afternoon.

Debating, she gazed at the park across the way. February in the South was being pushed to an early spring, and the flower bushes near her entryway displayed the first pink buds. Candee had assured Kathleen that a few more warm days and all the trees would be in bloom.

"Actually, I'm shattered," she said.

His thick eyebrows drew together. They were so close, she saw the threads of gray weaving between the dark hair.

"Exhausted," she explained. "More Irish slang. How about we just chat?"

"I'm up for that." He glanced at his watch, a high-priced brand she instantly recognized. "We can exchange classified information."

"This isn't Scotland Yard," she said. "And my commercial ovens haven't been installed yet, so I've been using the oven in my apartment to bake my breads."

"Will you show me around?"

She felt her cheeks heat. Her apartment? The setting was so intimate.

Aye, that was what he'd asked, and what she'd alluded to. The teahouse seemed the better choice, although kitchen equipment wouldn't begin arriving until Monday. And the large dough mixer was on back order. However, the vendor had assured it would arrive in plenty of time for her grand opening.

She shifted. She was fairly good at thinking on her feet and making quick decisions, but since Rob had arrived, the edges of the afternoon had blurred. Perhaps it was because she enjoyed being with him and hoped to impress him. Woefully, her place was the furthest one got from being impressive.

And he thought *he* was tongue-tied?

She rubbed her hands on her slacks, knowing he stared at her.

"Alright, then. Follow me upstairs," she said. "Before you arrived, I pulled loaves of my Irish breads and batches of scones out of the oven. I'd welcome your truthful opinion on the texture."

Rob seemed the kind of fella a woman could talk to. Despite his affluence, he seemed approachable. Who else wore a T-shirt advertising his company beneath a sport jacket?

She noticed there was no wedding band on the fourth finger of his left hand. Candee had offhandedly remarked he had never married. So he was alone in life, reminding Kathleen of herself.

"Lead the way, my beautiful Kathleen." He stepped nearer. "Have you ever sung, 'I'll Take You Home Again, Kathleen'? It's an Irish ballad."

"The song isn't Irish, Rob." She picked up the gift bag and ushered him around the building. "It has German-American origins."

"I memorized all the words. I'll sing it to you if you'd like."

Before she could answer, he belted out the melody in a smooth tenor voice, slightly out of tune, warbling lyrics about a wild ocean and a bonnie bride.

She laughed out loud, and it felt good to laugh with a friend, with a man.

Somehow, as they ascended the stairs, she knew she'd always remember this afternoon. The soft, promising breeze on her cheeks, the glint of a dipping sun changing her Carolina world to a silky, golden glow.

And the appealing grin on Rob's features that engaged his entire face. Women could be completely charmed by a man whose emotions were so utterly apparent. He literally wore his sentiments on his sleeve, much like the Irish.

They made their way to the top of the stairs, and he took her free hand as if it were the most natural thing in the world. When they reached the landing, he belted out the second verse, *I'll take you to your home again, Kathleen.*

She joined him, and they sang in unison.

CHAPTER FOUR

When they reached her apartment, they walked directly into her narrow, cozy kitchen as the screen door banged shut behind them. The floorboards creaked as she hung his jacket on a coat rack in the foyer.

The scent of yeast and sugar flavored the air, and Rob sniffed appreciatively. She invited him to sit at a wooden breakfast nook, consisting of corner unit benches and a table polished in a natural white finish and trimmed in yellow.

"Bread lies at the heart of Irish baking," Kathleen said. Efficiently, she sliced Irish soda bread and went to work on a loaf of brown bread. "Before we eat, let's pray a simple thanks to God." She bowed her head, and he did the same. She whispered a blessing, then offered him a portion of each bread.

The brown bread's crust was thick, the texture dense. The soda bread sprinkled with caraway seed tasted like a biscuit. Although hard on the outside, the inside was moist and delectable.

"Wonderful. I like them both." He helped himself to another two slices and washed them down with a bottle of water she'd pulled from the fridge.

"The trade secret is cooked raisins." She slid onto the bench across from him. "Save and freeze any leftover raisin water for a later batch. It will produce a sweeter flavor in the bread."

"I like trade secrets." *And he liked her.*

"Brown bread is a well-known Irish staple, so what I'm telling you isn't classified information. This bread is a treasured family recipe from my auntie Peggy."

Rob chewed and bobbed his head, encouraging her to continue.

"Auntie lived twenty days shy of her one hundredth birthday." Kathleen dashed tears from her eyes. "She was slim, walked everywhere all her life, and was witty and fun to be around."

"Do you miss her?" he asked quietly.

"Aye. She used to say that without a slab of brown bread every morning, no Irish kitchen is complete. In fact, you can't go into any pub or bakery without brown bread being on the menu."

"I've never visited Ireland." *Perhaps they could go together.*

"You'd love it." Wistfully, she sighed, although she didn't extend an invitation. "After drinking pints in a pub, this bread has saved my stomach at midnight on many occasions. Topped with a sliver of sharp cheddar cheese and heated in the broiler, it's delicious and not too heavy."

He carved another good-sized portion of bread for himself, slathered it with butter, and savored. Awe-inspiring. There were no other words for this woman's baked goods.

"I don't drink, and I'm old enough to admit I've learned a lot through the years," she said. "Giving up alcohol and nights at the pub were two of them. I've witnessed too much heartache. It's been estimated that at least half of all Irish drinkers are problem drinkers."

"Why such a large number?"

"The usual reasons." She looked away. "Affordability, ready availability, and heavy marketing."

"Are you referring to anyone in particular?" Gently cupping her chin in his hand, he directed her to face him.

"My employer, Danny Brady." She eased from Rob's grip, stood and surveyed a decorative ceramic platter in a glass cupboard before reaching for it. "Although not him, because he doesn't drink. His wife, Clara, has a brother who struggles with alcoholism." Kathleen's smoky eyes were remarkably expressive, filled with compassion. "Seamus was a dishwasher for a brief while at The Ground Café. He's been in and out of treatment programs since."

"How is he these days?"

She shrugged casually, a bit too casually considering her shoulders tightened. "Last I heard, he's back in treatment. Success rates for rehab are misleading and aren't as high as people expect."

"If you ever fancy a talk about Ireland, about anything, really, I'm a good listener," Rob said quietly.

"Fancy?" She reached beneath the end bench to a hidden storage unit and retrieved two sage-green place mats. "Is that an American term?"

"I'm trying out your Irish slang."

"*Fancy* is British English." She set the place mats on the table. "And I'll keep your offer in mind."

"Good." He broke the somber mood by gesturing to the counter overflowing with scones. Soon, he'd sampled her blueberry and plain scones baked to a golden-brown, proclaiming them exquisite. As Kathleen directed, he smeared a generous amount of butter and homemade strawberry jam on each.

He grinned. He liked taking directions from her.

Lulled by her lyrical Irish brogue, he listened to her jokes about Ireland's rainy weather and ran his hand down the bench's smooth pine finish. She had a discerning eye for design—it showed in her comfy, appealing kitchen. A leafy English ivy plant hung by the window, a cobalt-blue toaster splashed color on the counter, and a hand-woven rug in a creamy blue weave complemented the tile floor with texture.

"I like your sense of style," he said. "You must enjoy interior decorating."

"Hardly. I find decorating one challenge I prefer to leave to professionals." A smile bloomed on her face. "Tea? I'll put the kettle on."

"Sure."

"You're supposed to say *no, thanks*."

"I am? Why?"

"Because that's what is expected in an Irish home. No worries. We'll try again." Squarely, she faced him. "Tea?"

"No, thanks."

"Brilliant." She grinned, waited a beat. "Tea?"

"What's the correct answer? Yes?"

She pressed her lips needle thin.

"Aye?"

"Have you suddenly become Irish?" she asked.

"No?"

"Third time's a charm. Let's try once more." She smiled. "Tea?"

"Yes. That would be lovely." He folded his hands on his lap and watched her uncertainly.

"Very good."

"Whew." Dramatically, he wiped his brow. "I feel like I almost failed an algebra exam. Should I have started with a *cheerio*?"

"*Cheerio* is another British term and means farewell. Are you leaving?"

"I just arrived." His gaze flicked to the platter of brown bread and he grabbed another slice. "I sought the magic word, and the word *cheerio* always comes to mind when I think of you Brits."

With a heavy sigh, she bent to pick a crumb from the floor. "I'm from Dublin, which is part of the Republic of Ireland. We're our own country and not part of the UK. Shall I enlighten you on the differences between Northern Ireland and the Republic of Ireland?"

He steepled his fingers. "Certainly. I'm quite interested."

"That's a refreshing change. In the States, this topic doesn't often come up."

"I told you I'm an excellent listener." *Good. Excellent. Same difference.*

She seemed to digest his words before she spoke. "Let's get back to our tea discussion, shall we? In Ireland, it's customary to answer *no thanks* twice when offered tea. It's impolite to say *yes* until the third ask." She took a breath. "Once more for practice. Ready?"

He gave a thumbs-up, considered including the word *aye*, but didn't.

"Tea?" she asked.

He held up one finger, then two, mouthing the numbers. "I assume I'm safe because this is at least the third try."

"It's actually the first because we were trying again," she said. "I'll let it pass, though."

"Then I'd love a cup of tea, thank you."

"Cuppa."

"Cup of."

She laughed. "Soon you'll get the hang of it. Are you ready for more questions?"

"Sure."

"Do you prefer milk and sugar? Or a squeeze of lemon?"

"My choice is black tea with lots of sugar." His mouth

twitched in amusement as she approved. "I see you Irish take your tea quite seriously," he added.

"Aye, which is why I'd like to teach Americans how to serve a proper tea." She put water in a kettle and placed it on the stove. While waiting for the water to boil, she retrieved two china cups, saucers, and a matching creamer and sugar bowl embellished with blue flowers. She poured milk into the creamer, added lumps of sugar to the open jar, and arranged china and linen napkins on the table.

He considered telling her that if she spent that long preparing each customer's cup of tea, she'd never earn a profit. Instead, he wisely opted for keeping silent as she poured the boiling water into the teapot and their two teacups.

"This warms the pot and our cups," she explained. She waited a minute before discarding the water from the pot and cups into the sink. Then she added two tea bags into the teapot and poured in boiling water.

While he encouraged her to talk about her vision for the teahouse, they filled their plates with more bread. She kept an eye on her wristwatch in between nibbles. After three minutes, she removed the tea bags to an extra plate, stirred the tea, and glided onto the bench.

"First draw?" she asked, preparing to pour.

"I prefer a dark tea."

"Me too." Quickly, she added the tea bags back to the pot for another minute. "A favorite Irish expression is, *strong enough to trot a mouse in* for dark tea."

"Clever. I suggest you not use that expression around your customers, though."

"Mice in the kitchen. The idea would definitely keep patrons away." Her face lightened with wry laughter. "Did you realize the Irish aren't the world's biggest consumer of tea?"

"Who is? England?"

She shook her head. "Turkey, then Ireland, then the UK."

For the next few minutes, he considered voicing his views on buying and selling, and keeping an eye on profit margin. Because he was a competent entrepreneur, he assumed his advice would be welcomed with enthusiasm.

Painstakingly, she poured the tea.

"Thank you." He relished the rich, deep flavor and smiled. They sat silently for a few minutes, savoring their tea.

"If I opened a teahouse," he said, "I'd insert those attention-grabbing tidbits you shared about tea preparation on the menu. Items of interest will enhance your customers' experience and provide them with something to talk about beyond your delectable desserts."

"Maybe." She stared straight ahead while he sipped. Finally, she said, "I'm glad you like tea."

He hadn't said if he liked tea. In fact, he preferred coffee, even over this exquisite brew. But tea was apparently the Irish way, and he sat back on the wooden bench and warmed his fingers around the fragile china cup. Inhaling the fragrant steam, he plated another sliver of brown bread. "Candee was dead-on. Your baked goods are outstanding. And your scones—"

"Thanks. Coming from you, I'm flattered."

"My cupcakes and muffins aren't anywhere near as exciting as your Irish brown bread." He downed the rest of his tea. "I'm thinking about selling fancier pastries in my bakeries. Every one of them needs a face-lift, and foods not normally experienced in standard American shops might benefit sales. Currently, my blueberry muffins are customer favorites. Mind if I pick your brain for innovative European recipes?"

"Certainly. I'm delighted to share what I know." She placed her teacup on her saucer with a clink. "However, if you're turning a grand profit, which I assume you are judging from what Candee has said, why change anything? My ideas aren't any better than yours."

His instinct was to volley her comment back to her while reciting the adage *two heads are better than one*, or some such sage proverb.

However, that wasn't entirely true. The truth was, he wanted to spend time with her, because he could hardly tear his gaze away from her striking face, her delicate smile. She looked utterly gorgeous, her porcelain complexion flushed from a veil of steamy tea.

Mentally, he went over his flight details, suddenly loathe to leave Roses on Tuesday morning. Maybe he'd stay a few extra days, go sightseeing with her, dine with her at the farm-to-table restaurant Candee and Teddy raved about.

"Would you like to see Asheville with me tomorrow afternoon?" he blurted.

"I can't spare the time, although I'm sure Asheville is splendid." Kathleen busied herself with pouring another round of tea. "After March seventeenth, well, perhaps then. Although you don't live here so timing might be difficult."

"I come to Roses often."

"Do you?"

He'd come more now, even if it meant leaving his precious bakeries in the hands of his assistant managers. And to his amazement, he was okay with that.

"By plane, Miami to Asheville is less than a three-hour flight," he said.

"Rob—"

He couldn't gauge her expression beyond that one sharp word. Was she not interested? Preoccupied?

"I'm just saying," he said. "We can exchange phone numbers, alright? In case you need to text me about anything."

"Sure." She gave him her cell-phone number.

He sent her a quick text. *Hi. I'm Rob. 1-800-IRELAND.*

Her smile expanded as she scanned his message. "What does that mean?"

"It means you can call me toll free anytime you need my help and never incur a charge."

She grinned. "I'll remember that. In the meantime—" her voice quieted, seeming to soften her refusal—"I want to stand out with an exceptional product so people will flock to my place. What do you judge to be the best ...?"

So she sought his opinion after all, although she'd adeptly sidestepped any personal conversation. When they focused on shop talk, her eyes lit with enthusiasm.

And while they faced each other in her inviting kitchen, he realized something extraordinary. His heart, cold for so long, was thawing. He loved a woman with enthusiasm, and her obvious excitement about her business ignited her smile. He saw the evidence in her dark, gleaming eyes and the way she sat straighter, gesturing with her hands. Her grin widened, displaying white, even teeth. She was already striking. When she elaborated on her innovative concepts, she was altogether alluring.

In turn, she fanned a spark in him he thought had been extinguished long ago.

"... vegan baked goods using organic products," she was saying. "What do you think, Rob?"

What did he think about what? He'd been too preoccupied with gazing at her.

"Rob, were you listening?"

"Of course."

"What did I say?"

"You were mentioning using ground flax meal in your ... scones."

"Aye, that was ten minutes ago."

"People are opting for a wider variety of choices, so consider customers' lifestyle choices when figuring out your menu." He searched his mind for topics he'd discussed with his managers through the years, and added, "Currently, I'm serving carbohydrates, fats, sugar, and caffeine in my shops, so obviously my menus are on the fattening side."

"It's all a balancing act, isn't it?" she asked.

"Life?"

"I was referring to food, but aye, I suppose life too." Pensively, she regarded him, then fished through a kitchen drawer and came back with two sheets of paper and pencils. "How about we combine taste with nutrition?"

We.

"Don't forget your bottom line," he said. "Otherwise, you'll be out of business within six months."

She seemed not to have heard him, intent on her list-making, mouthing the words as she penned them. "Craveability," she wrote with a flourish, then pursed her lips. "Is that a word?"

"It is now. And it's a good one."

"Are you interested in going over my business plan with me step by step?" she asked.

"Can I ask you a question first?"

"Aye."

"Have you begun interviewing applicants?"

"No. I'm running an ad in the local paper soon. If I get stuck, Sean, a coworker in Ireland, has offered to assist me."

"How generous," Rob said sardonically.

"He's a dependable manager, and versed in the restaurant business."

"So he's willing to quit his job in Ireland to fly here to help you?"

"Aye."

"There's plenty of suitable workers here in the US." Rob lifted his pencil off the paper. "Should I start listing my ideas?"

"Aye. Fill up the whole sheet."

A thought struck him. Actually two thoughts.

Without admitting it, she'd concurred that two brains were, in fact, better than one. And any comparing of recipes wouldn't be done that evening. He'd already established that anything baked in her oven came out superb.

He tapped his pencil while she wrote an extensive list in a scholarly penmanship he hadn't seen in ages. Nowadays, everyone typed on their computers.

Soon, her list crammed both sides of the paper.

She nibbled the end of her pencil. "This is too much," she murmured. "I'll never complete all these tasks."

"Have you considered prioritizing?" He skimmed the tasks and numbered them according to importance. "And let's pare down this list. You can do that, right?"

"Aye." She consented, humming a familiar Irish folk song, "Oh Danny Boy", under her breath, as she crossed out a word and added alternates.

Hours later, when he gazed through her sheer white kitchen curtains, a full, round moon sailed high in the sky. He glanced at his wristwatch in amazement. The hours spent with her had been nothing short of delightful.

She was a stunningly attractive woman. A woman who touched something powerful and unfamiliar inside him.

Lifting his cell-phone from his pocket, he texted Teddy.

Pick me up at ten, Rob typed.

Did your two hours change to six? came Teddy's reply. *Glad U R enjoying your evening. We were wondering what happened.*

Worried about me?

Always.

I'm fine, Rob typed.

More than fine.

Across the table, Kathleen smiled at him, and Rob's heart did a little meltdown.

Because she's remarkable.

Rob finished his message to Teddy and clicked send.

CHAPTER FIVE

Although he tried, Rob couldn't convince Kathleen to play hooky and accompany him to Asheville. She refused, and with good reason considering her opening date of March 17. Instead of sightseeing on his own, he shelved the idea until his next visit, assuring her that he was more than happy to assist her.

While she spent Monday morning securing a line of credit and visiting warehouses, Rob followed breakfasting with Candee and Teddy to lunching at O'Malley's pub, where he assumed head waiter relief for a harried Desiree and Keiran. Pleased the pub appeared busy and profitable, Rob walked the short distance to the teahouse.

Although spring hadn't technically arrived on the calendar, pale lavender crocuses burst through the soil in backyard gardens, and a lazy breeze swept across the grass. Rob plunged his hands into the pockets of his gray windbreaker, delighting in the fresh air against his face. Roses' weather made him feel more animated than he'd felt in ages. February and March were transitional months in Miami, heralding a brief spring before the intense summer heat arrived.

Admittedly, the bounce in his step had more to do with a certain Irishwoman than the temperate weather, his comfortable jeans, or tennis shoes.

As he strolled at a brisk pace, Rob mulled Kathleen's comment from the previous evening.

It's all a balancing act, isn't it?

Yes, he thought. You're so wise. For years, he'd sought to appease thousands of patrons—tweaking recipes, solving every complaint, adhering to the adage "the customer is always right". He'd been so focused on developing his business, he'd pushed aside any notion of personal happiness.

Love? Nope, not even a blip on his radar screen.

Armed with painful past experiences, he struggled to recall why love was so important—why poets wrote sonnets, why it made the world go round.

Because love was everything. Because love mattered above all else.

"Ridiculous notion," he whispered. Besides, he was too old for love. And Kathleen ... well, when he calculated their age difference, he came up with fifteen years.

Had it always been so clear, so straightforward, these unspoken rules for dating and romance? Certainly, problematic circumstances occurred, although Candee encouraged his interest in Kathleen. She'd sensed it immediately, sniffed it out like one of her beloved beagles. In fact, he and Candee had discussed Kathleen throughout breakfast while Teddy looked on with amusement.

Before Rob left, Candee suggested that Kathleen join them for an intimate evening get-together at her home.

"Don't forget to tell Kathleen dinner is at six," Candee reminded as Rob ducked out the door and settled into Teddy's pickup for a ride to town. "And, Rob, a May-December romance is just the thing when two people are so attracted to each other."

He'd given a brief nod, neither agreeing nor disagreeing, although he'd googled age-gap couples on the internet. Studies showed these couples were extremely happy despite social disapproval.

Still, he felt as if his searches let him down, as the findings had encouraged dreams he'd catalogued as unattainable. He wasn't about to fall in love with anyone, including the beautiful Kathleen. Anyone who knew him could recite his unsuccessful dating record. Regardless of his wealth and achievements, women left him flat, and it hurt more than he admitted. No woman chose a man with a retreating hairline (he was being kind to himself—the correct term was bald), and a waistline that increased with every passing year. More important, the sting of heartbreak was too steep an expense for a few weeks of happiness.

When he rounded the last curve to the teahouse, Rob was out of breath from the final rise in the road. Beneath the overhang of the wide front porch, Kathleen paced impatiently, coming to a stop as if she'd sensed his arrival.

"Hi, Rob." She scratched the back of her neck, her shoulders tight. "I'm relieved you're here."

He puffed to a halt. "Anything wrong?"

"I'm waiting for a distributor to ring me about the oven delivery. I admit I'm terribly impatient. And the large dough mixer is still on back order."

"Sometimes things move slower in the South," he said.

"The same holds true for Ireland." She sighed heavily. "I've been known to snap at people if they're late. I don't want a reputation in the States for being rude. Folks in Ireland accused me of bad behavior on more than one occasion, and I was ashamed and apologized."

"You're a person who likes to get things done. I'm the same way."

Her shoulders relaxed. "Thanks for the assurance."

He caught his breath at the sight of her. That smile. Those deep-brown eyes. He knew he'd think about her every minute of his flight back to Florida. Pausing, he remarked favorably on the exterior of the building, the white glossy trim and exposed brick.

"Teddy's crew is painting the interior and exterior," she said. "He provided a generous bid I couldn't refuse. They started this morning and accomplished a lot already."

"What was his bid? Thousands of dollars?"

"He's offering the labor for free. I'm paying for materials."

"Another reason why I always liked him," Rob joked. He chased ideas across his mind. How could he top Teddy's generosity?

"Please, please come in," she said. The screen door groaned on its hinges as she guided him inside. He envisioned how the diner had been situated—the long counter and various booths were still waiting to be removed. The greasy cooktop hadn't been cleaned in years. On the walls were large black square marks where paintings had once hung.

"The place looks ... good," he said. He searched for another word and couldn't find it.

She winced. "Surely, you're joking." She meandered, pointing out wet stains on the ceiling, bemoaning the former owner who had left the windows open, subsequently leading to water damage on the ceiling.

They stepped across the linoleum floor, coated in thick layers of dust.

Amidst the constant pounding of hammers, an Irish band played "When Irish Eyes Are Smiling" on a CD player. Sounding as if the song had been recorded in a pub, the rousing chorus prompted Rob to sing along.

"You recognize this tune?" she asked.

"Doesn't everyone? Irish music is well-known around the world."

She grinned. "I'm proud to be Irish."

"And I'm proud to know you. You're a resourceful entrepreneur."

"You're a grand fella, just like Candee said."

He chuckled.

"Am I turning scarlet this very minute?" she asked. "For complimenting you?"

They stared at each other in comfortable silence. "A little," he admitted.

She burst into laughter. "Well, that's settled then. Crack on."

"Get to work?"

"Aye."

The blue vinyl seating had been torn out and sat in a heap by the back door. Gingerly, they stepped around it.

"I'm baffled about pricing the scones competitively and hope you can brainstorm with me," she said.

"I'll try, but I should warn you. As I grow older, I'm baffled more often than not."

"About scones?"

"About life in general."

She grinned. "Right, well, welcome to my life too."

She had twisted her strawberry-blond hair into a semblance of a bun, securing the hairdo with pins and a shiny green ribbon. The pulled-back style accentuated her high cheekbones and dainty chin. Her wide eyes seemed too large for her refined features, and the swingy striped T-shirt and baggy sweatpants reflected her commitment to hard work, not to being a slave to the latest fashion.

Once at an empty booth, Kathleen plunged into ordering kitchen equipment, leaving little time for chitchat save for her sharp questions. He pulled off his windbreaker, rolled up his sleeves, and sat across from her.

"Tea?" she finally asked.

"Oh no. Will it be an all-day process?"

"Only a few minutes, I promise. And I'll take your answer as an *aye*." She climbed the interior steps to her apartment and came back carrying a tray chock full of stoneware—cups, a teapot filled with steaming tea, sugar and creamer, and scones from the previous evening.

Today she wasn't glamorous. Today she was simply breathtaking. Despite her flushed cheeks, her complexion was bone-white, revealing dark shadows under her eyes. Bound by the invisible strands of a strong work ethic, he'd later look back on the afternoon as the best he'd spent in decades.

In between her visiting with suppliers who stopped in and a meeting with a service rep, he inquired about her years as head assistant for Danny Brady. He even pressed for information about her dating past, to be sure no man waited for her in Ireland.

Her responses were vague, although she revealed she'd dated a couple fellas and discovered both were liars. Actually, she used the word *eejit*.

"These days, I'm embarrassed I was a stook for believing them," she said.

"*Stook* is another Irish word for idiot?"

"Aye." She wove her fingers together and glanced at the floor.

By late afternoon one of the ovens had been delivered, and the last of Teddy's crew packed his tools and left. She stepped over to a rusty sink to wash her hands for the umpteenth time, and Rob came beside her.

"I'm leaving tomorrow," he reminded. "I hope you'll join me for dinner tonight at Candee and Teddy's house."

She wrenched the faucet shut. "Is that an invite?"

"A sincere invite."

"I'm sorry." Her expression became pensive. "I wish, but I'm drowning here."

"I'm wishing too." He wished he could stay in Roses. Another day, another two days. She hadn't encouraged him, although he'd dropped several broad hints.

He decided to take matters into his own hands. He couldn't help himself.

Gently, he brought her to face him. Before she could reply, he bent his head and kissed her, a feather-light touch of his lips to hers.

She tasted of tea and sugar, her fragrance the subtle scent of lavender.

At first, she didn't move. When his hand curved around her back and the kiss deepened, she broke free.

"Obviously," she said, "we're not going to start dating."

"Why?"

"Because you live in Miami. And I live in Ire ... I mean, Roses."

"That's why they invented airplanes. And cell-phones."

She moved backward. "You, of all people, should know I'm not interested, given you've heard my dating history."

"So you dated a few guys who were rogues. Not all of us are like that."

"*Rogue* is a harsh word." Her reddish-brown eyebrows lifted. "Is the term American?"

"I've never used the word before. I assumed it was British, and I was trying to impress you."

"Irish. I'm Irish." She gazed at him and her smile came slow, lighting her heart-shaped face. She was delightful—part cherub and part tigress. His heart beat in double-time.

"My dating track record wouldn't win any awards, either," he said quietly.

She studied him.

Fearful she might feel sorry for him, an old guy, a desperate bachelor, he waved a hand indifferently. "I'm only telling you so we can commiserate."

"About love and romance?"

"About commonality. We both target accomplishment above all else."

"From the sounds of it, we're both workaholics."

The quiet lasted several beats, punctuated only by the drip, drip, drip of a tarnished faucet.

"You know, I could use someone like you in my bakeries," he said. "Someone energetic and organized."

"*Your* bakeries?" Her Irish brogue thickened. "In Miami?"

"Yes. You'd like Miami. It's—" He'd been about to say it was hot and humid before stopping himself. He certainly couldn't illustrate a Miami travel brochure if those were the only adjectives coming to mind.

She plunked her fists on her hips. "As you are certainly aware, I have my own business right here in Roses."

"How could I forget?" He tugged on his windbreaker. "We've dreamt up a million ideas about it all afternoon."

"Don't you understand? I need to do this on my own."

"I understand that you won't allow me to help you."

"By giving everything up? Why would you ask me such a question?"

Because he didn't want to leave her. And he couldn't just abandon his businesses. Hers was just starting up. Perhaps she could sell the diner. Or the teahouse. Or whatever she preferred to call it.

Thankfully, he kept his opinions to himself, for when he rotated, he confronted narrowed eyes and a stormy expression.

"You'd learn a lot," he said, "and I'd promote you to a manager in my flagship Miami bakery."

"Surely, you're joking. *Flagship* was my middle name in Dublin. Been there, done that."

"You won't earn a decent salary here for months, maybe even years."

Definitely the wrong thing to say, judging by the anger flashing from her dark eyes.

"Haven't you heard a word in all the hours we've spent together? My answer is no. Absolutely not." She spun and gathered up the stoneware, placing cups and teapot on the tray.

"What about this evening's invite?" he asked. "Candee and Teddy are expecting us."

"Tell them I'll probably see them tomorrow." She picked up the tray. "You may not live in Roses, Rob, but I do."

"I can stick around a few more hours. Really. I'll text Teddy and—"

"No. We're done here." Resolutely, she shook her head. "Enjoy the flight back to Miami and thanks for your help."

CHAPTER SIX

The following morning, Kathleen was awakened by persistent hammering coming from the floor below her apartment. The sun poured into her bedroom window and she checked the time, knowing she'd overslept.

After a quick shower, she gulped some tea and hastened downstairs.

The five crewmen who greeted her caused her to stop short. All the scene needed was a foreman. As the word came to mind, Teddy appeared. In a lazy southern drawl, he adeptly guided the men to sheetrock, sand and paint. As he joked with them, she could hardly believe he ran such a large construction firm, because he was so laid-back.

Of course, the same held true for Rob. His winning smile was disarming, and he'd been heralded as Miami's most successful entrepreneur.

His dry humor was comfortable, cheerful, and concise. After he'd abruptly left the day before, her reflections continued to revolve around him. Not her business plan, nor her scones, nor a proper cuppa. Just him.

"Good morning, Kathleen." Candee waved from the

doorway of the back room. "Teddy and I came to see how your place is progressing."

Kathleen sucked in her bottom lip. "Good as gold, thanks to Teddy."

"It's a virtual circus around here, but a good sign because it means things are moving quickly."

"Aye." Kathleen fidgeted with the skirt of the apron she'd thrown over her jeans and charcoal-gray sweatshirt. She knew she looked a sight and slanted a glance toward the workers. By way of an explanation, she said, "I was experimenting with a new recipe for scones last night, and went to bed later than I planned."

"You're worn out."

"Knackered is the Irish word."

"Have you eaten breakfast?"

"Black tea."

Candee waved several brown bags in the air. "You must eat a decent meal or you'll fade away. Teddy and I brought you a typical southern breakfast, but I won't take credit for the cooking. Grits and eggs, buttermilk biscuits and sausage swimming in creamy white gravy, compliments of Keiran."

"Thank you. I haven't had the chance to meet him yet."

"As you're aware, he has family in Dublin so you'll have lots to chat about." Candee flashed a sunny grin. "C'mon. Let's eat."

"I won't be able to fit into any of my clothes," Kathleen warned, while Candee led her through the back room, littered with debris. By the window facing the yard, they assembled at a three-legged table salvaged from the diner. A chest of drawers Kathleen had brought from Ireland held some of her personal belongings.

Candee brought out warm food wrapped in foil containers, complete with silverware and cloth napkins. For herself, she set carry-out coffee and sugar packets on the table.

"I assume you drink tea," Candee said as she poured three packets of sugar into her coffee and stirred.

"I've had my fill for now." Kathleen pulled a bottled water from the cooler.

She perched at the end of the booth, gestured for Candee to sit across from her, and said a blessing. Although she'd baked, she hadn't prepared a proper meal for herself since she'd arrived.

"I'm sorry you weren't able to join us last night," Candee said over the rim of her coffee cup.

Kathleen helped herself to another forkful of eggs. Candee had bragged about Keiran's cooking with obvious good reason.

"I'm hoping for a raincheck," she said. "I'd love to see your home."

"Rob missed you."

Kathleen felt her cheeks color. "We had a slight disagreement."

"He was unusually quiet at dinner."

Thinking over his offer tugged hard on Kathleen's mood, and she took a deep breath. "He assumed I'd prefer to work for him rather than run my own business."

"He said that?"

"He suggested I become a manager at his bakery in Miami. Why on earth would—?" Kathleen broke off.

"Only one reason."

"Which is?" After studying Candee's determined features, Kathleen sensed the answer. "You think this was his way of us being together?"

"Are you ... together?"

"We met a few days ago. Surely you don't believe we're falling in love."

With a bemused smile, Candee said, "Why do you think

people call it falling in love? Love develops quickly and feels like you're losing control. You know—falling, tripping—"

Kathleen dismissed this with a head shake. "I'm not seeking any type of courtship. Too often, I've failed in the dating department. I'm good at business. Strictly business."

She wasn't an obsessed, clingy woman who needed a man. At least, not anymore.

Nonchalantly, Candee sipped her coffee. "Every person is different. You'll know when the right man comes along."

Like Rob, for instance?

No. Not happening.

Blankly, Kathleen stared at the paneled wall behind Candee. Admittedly, thoughts of Rob consumed her. He made her feel relaxed and encouraged, telling her she could handle the most difficult situation. And he'd made it clear he was available.

She heaved a breath. At this rate, she was focusing more hours and energy on him than her teahouse. How would she ever create a tea emporium if she couldn't even manage to get menus finalized?

"Why don't men ever listen to women?" she asked.

"Because men and women are wired differently," Candee replied. "Knowing Rob, he was only trying to help. He doesn't understand why you should struggle when he can do so much for you."

"He said that?"

"Yes."

"I know he believes in me," Kathleen said. "Now I want him to stand back so I can face the challenges on my own."

"He's a man who looks at a problem and presents a solution. He's practical. Once you learn more about him, you'll understand."

Oh, but she had learned about him. Beneath their light bantering she'd discovered he'd never married and wasn't currently dating. Beneath his laughter, she felt certain he'd been hurt. On their first night, he'd revealed his home life had been filled with rejection. His parents had never responded favorably to his bids for affection and hadn't approved of his profession.

There was more. She knew there was more, although he hadn't spoken of it. Perhaps someday. At present, she wouldn't push, wouldn't pry. Besides, when would she see him again?

Beneath his commanding exterior she sensed an easily bruised sensitivity. And with that insight, she was more attracted to him. Because he was vulnerable, just like her. Sometimes the most prosperous men were the most insecure. Perhaps it was the reason why he was driven to succeed.

She stared out the window. Sunlight exposed floating dust particles. A fluorescent light bulb buzzed overhead, calling attention to the discolored ceiling.

"The thing is," Kathleen said, "Rob is fun to be around. He's well-educated and freely shares his experience."

"When Teddy needed a friend, Rob was there. He's loyal and generous." At Kathleen's inquisitive expression, Candee added, "The next time he comes to Roses, you might see his generosity in action. He's involved in several charitable organizations, including one with Keiran."

"Rob comes to Roses often?"

Candee grinned. "He will now."

Kathleen's heart swelled. When Rob had smiled at her, kissed her, she'd felt a shiny spin of hope. Perhaps here, in America ...

No. She refused to dwell on a future that could never be. If she and Rob dated, she knew the ending. Men left her without a care. Every single time.

She concentrated on the last of her biscuit and white

gravy. Some people were meant to live life alone. She was one of them.

"And do you know why?" Candee asked.

"Know why what?" Kathleen glanced up, noting Candee's mischievous grin. "Why Rob will be back? Do you know something I don't?"

"Me?" Candee feigned an expression so innocent, Kathleen burst out laughing. "He talked about you the entire evening and kept looking at his phone," Candee went on. "I think he was hoping you'd reconsidered our invite."

"I couldn't." Kathleen stood and threw open the window to let in some fresh air. "Look around."

"You sent him back to Miami with your rejection." Accusation colored Candee's voice.

Kathleen bristled. "Wasn't he leaving, anyway? He owns a half-dozen bakeries."

"He wanted to stay longer. In fact, he'd been in touch with his Miami assistant manager."

Kathleen knew her cheeks colored. Aye, her refusal had been blunt, but she'd worked for others her entire life. Wasn't sacrificing all those sweat-filled years enough?

"I didn't mean to hurt his feelings, although I doubt he was affected," she said.

"Did you apologize?"

"What?" Kathleen's eyes widened. "He should apologize to me."

Candee settled her elbows on the table and rested her chin on her fists. "Have you heard from him?"

"He texted me last night." Again, Kathleen stared out the window at the post-card perfect sky.

The previous afternoon, she and Rob had tossed designs around. Their conversation had been easy, and she hadn't laughed so hard in years. She'd been impressed with his quick mind, the ease in which he'd presented practical, timely solutions to her questions, writing extensive lists with his bold left-handed scrawl.

"What did he say in his texts?" Candee asked.

"He said he enjoyed his time with me. I wished him a safe flight," Kathleen said.

"Unfortunately, you're both too polite."

Kathleen took note of Candee's set jaw. "Meaning?"

"You didn't discuss what really matters."

"Dating?" Kathleen clenched her hands together. "When I'm drowning in business loan debt?"

"Love is the only thing that matters."

"Maybe in your world. Certainly not in mine. What matters is that I'm starting a brand-new venture and can't concentrate on anything else."

Candee doctored her coffee with another packet of sugar and took a long swallow. "I admit Rob is a little high-handed at times."

"It's because he's skilled and on the ball. And funny and warm-hearted."

Exactly what the other men in her life had lacked. In the short days they'd known each other, Rob had displayed a tenderness she hadn't noticed at first, developing in the course of their hours together. She'd listened as he'd laughingly remarked about his dismal dating history. Although he'd airily portrayed himself as a man who couldn't care less, his admission seemed more heartbreaking than humorous.

"Wow, Kathleen." Candee set down her cup. "You're quick to come to his defense."

"I—" Kathleen rubbed her palms on her sweatshirt.

"I see you're interested in him. It's written all over your face. Admit it."

Kathleen averted her eyes from Candee's attentive gaze. Despite her exhaustion, she hadn't slept well. If she had more time, she might have talked further about Rob, but the sentences wedged in her throat. Unfortunately, time was something she lacked, and life went on.

She walked back to the table and dabbed her lips with her napkin. "What interests me is designing this blank space into a charming teahouse in a few short weeks." As she disposed of the containers, Candee wrapped the silverware and napkins.

Through the doorway, Teddy and his crew set up ladders, arranged tools and prepared joint compound.

Kathleen perused the bare walls. She'd never considered interior decorating her strong suit despite Rob's compliments. In any case, he'd only seen her kitchen.

"How can I best utilize every inch of space?" she asked aloud.

"This is where I come in." Candee popped to her feet.

For the next several hours, Candee shared design tips while drawing up a floor plan, adding extra windows and laying out a well-equipped kitchen complete with sinks, a cooler, and oven placement. When Kathleen peered over Candee's shoulder, Candee said, "No worries. I'm keeping in mind the strict health code."

Meanwhile, Kathleen grabbed scrubbing supplies and tackled the shelving.

When they finished, Candee locked arms with Kathleen and yanked her out the front door. "And now, we're going shopping."

"My pantry is stocked with flour and baking soda."

"Good, because we're canvassing all the paint stores for samples. Fun bright colors will look terrific on the interior walls, and I suggest leaving the exposed brick behind the counter. Build a fireplace on the far wall with a wide pine mantel."

"Let's section the rooms to keep them more intimate," Kathleen said. "The smaller room can seat ten to twelve people, the larger up to twenty. I want worn leather couches in the sitting area, a loveseat, and blackboard by the entrance so I can chalk in the soups of the day." A wave of excitement coursed through her as more ideas took hold. "Creamy broccoli or parsnips with apple and curry are favorite soups in Ireland."

"Parsnips?" Candee asked. "What are those?"

"A root vegetable similar to a carrot, only cream-colored."

"When parsnip soup is on your menu, call me," Candee said. "Now, over and above food, let's get back to decorating. Stripping the wood on the sideboards will create an antique feel."

"At some point, I'll need a taste tester for the scones and bread."

Candee paused. "Is that all you think about—food?"

"I own a teahouse, not a bookstore."

Candee gazed at her with an overly satisfied expression. "I know the ideal person for the job."

"Who?"

"Rob."

Kathleen's pulse skipped a beat. The subject, the man she'd avoided talking about all afternoon, brought a smile she couldn't contain.

"Aye," she agreed.

Did her enthusiasm make her look transparent? The twinkle in Candee's eyes gave Kathleen her answer.

Aye.

CHAPTER SEVEN

Rob stood in the backyard of Candee and Teddy's Victorian mansion, gazing at the enclosed pasture. Teddy had converted a large shed into a stable and purchased a Haflinger horse, sturdy and energetic with a flaxen mane, for Joseph's therapy.

When Joseph got off the school bus, Rob was propped against the fence admiring the home's gingerbread trim, which Candee had painted burnt-sienna. The shade nicely offset the mustard color exterior.

"Mr. Rob!" Joseph squealed in delight as he charged down the driveway. "I'm so happy you're back in Roses!" Out of breath, he dropped his bookbag on the ground and launched into Rob's arms. "How long will you stay?"

Rob managed a jovial smile. "A few days, maybe more."

Maybe less. It all depended on how a certain beautiful Irishwoman responded when he showed up at her teahouse.

After Candee had phoned him, breathless with the news that Kathleen had spoken favorably about him, she'd used her finest singsong voice and urged him to return to Roses. That took some planning, but he'd assembled his managers and arranged the necessary details.

"I'm only a phone call away," he'd assured, with the unspoken hope no one rang.

So here he was, a week later, back in Roses. This time, he vowed not to talk shop with Kathleen. At least, not *his* shop. He was here merely to lend a hand.

As the opening drew nearer, she might fly into a panic. Consequently, he was ready and able to offer his support.

"Mr. Rob, what do you think of my horse?" Joseph tipped his head toward the small horse being led out of the stable by the therapist.

"I think your horse is awesomely pint-sized," Rob said.

"His name is Blackjack," Joseph said with an impish smile.

Nearing seven years old, the little boy had quickly emerged from a preschooler to a thriving second grader. The freckles on his cheeks were disappearing and baby teeth had begun to fall out, leaving a gap-toothed grin.

"Yes, I know. Even though Blackjack is chestnut colored and not at all black."

"Blackjack doesn't mind." Joseph's face shone with happiness. "He likes his name."

Rob touched the boy's chin. "I'm sure he does."

Teddy and Candee's love and affection had strengthened the boy's self-esteem, and he bore little resemblance to the broken child Rob remembered from a few years earlier.

"Rob?" Teddy called from the back porch. "Are you ready? Kathleen's expecting you." Thumbs hooked in his front jean pockets, he grinned indulgently. Whenever he spoke to Rob about Kathleen, he smirked. Just like Candee did.

"Be right there," Rob said.

"I've gotta go too, Mr. Rob." With a breeze tangling his fine hair and an eager smile on his face, Joseph scampered away.

A few minutes later, Rob arrived at the teahouse. In several days, the exterior had been transformed from drab to grand. The old-world appearance Kathleen strived for conveyed a welcoming invitation to passersby. Her signage, Kathleen's Teahouse, stained in lavender and blues and exaggerated by pink teacups, had been fixed high above the entrance.

His gaze roamed enthusiastically over the renovated building. Afternoon had settled, and the windows were aglow with lit electric candles.

A very welcoming place indeed. He just hoped the owner's heart held the same welcome.

Watching through lowered lashes, Kathleen stood on her front porch as Rob got out of Teddy's pickup and waved a thanks. The work crew had retired for the day and the house was empty. They began at seven in the morning and clocked out at three thirty, so without the constant rat-a-tat-tat of hammering, the hollowness echoing through the rooms was oppressive.

"Cheers," she greeted Rob as he approached. "It's good to see you."

"A greeting from a beautiful woman is the best form of welcome," he said.

She smiled. "The Irish are known for their hospitality." As much as she tried, she couldn't tamp down the flurry in her chest at seeing him again.

Should they embrace like great friends, erasing their silly squabble? He had texted an apology and she'd done the same. Since then, the subject of her moving to Miami hadn't been broached. Thankfully, that had been settled.

She kept her hands at her sides while considering what to do next.

"It's good to see you again too." His blue eyes were steady and genial, startlingly intense. His tan golf shirt fit his frame perfectly, and he carried himself as a self-assured man, not a young guy who'd disguised his identity on the internet. Rob's tastes were sophisticated, and he was cultured and witty, an enticing combination.

No doubt about it. No matter how she resisted, she was drawn to him.

An expression of unconcealed admiration touched his handsome face. "I came back for you."

"Because of me, or for me?"

"Both."

"Did you assume I needed help, or did you want to see me?"

"Both."

"So you're not here to sightsee or visit friends?"

"I'm here exclusively for you." Warmly, he appraised her. "And you look gorgeous."

"Gorgeous? Hardly." Self-consciously, she patted her hair and offered a fatigued smile. Then she tugged at the pinstriped blouse and dark-washed jeans she'd changed into after a quick shower. Rob had texted saying when he'd arrive, but, as usual, she hadn't allowed enough time for herself and had settled for braiding her hair and applying pink lip gloss.

"Kathleen." He stepped closer. "I missed you. And I want you to know how much."

"You've only been gone a short while."

"The days were long for me."

The heat in her cheeks became a full-blown fire. Her gaze dropped to the flowers he held.

"I missed you too," she said quietly.

Attraction was a funny thing. It made you forget about feigning disinterest, a game suited for years thankfully well past.

"These are for you." He offered the flowers. "I asked the florist in town for something Irish."

"They're lovely." Kathleen accepted the bouquet of fresh-cut green and white button mums and carnations, the perfumed fragrance reminding her of the bushy plants growing wild in County Galway.

Her beloved Ireland. Nostalgia rushed through her, clogging her throat with emotion.

"Thank you," she managed.

"Are you homesick?"

"A little, although it's childish." Her eyes turned liquid, and a tear streaked down her cheek. "This is what I wanted—America and my own business. Fortunately, I've kept myself so busy my mind doesn't have time to wander."

Gently, he brushed the tear away. "I'm here and not going anywhere. Teddy and Candee said I can stay at their house as long as I'd like."

"What about your bakeries?"

"My marvelous muffins are so marvelous they practically bake themselves."

Despite herself, she chuckled.

He took the flowers from her, set them on the porch's wide railing, and gathered her into his arms.

She'd dreamt of this moment ever since they'd parted, and she didn't resist. Instead, she pressed her cheek along the smooth cotton of his shirt. The steady beating of his heart reassured her that he was here, truly here. And all was well.

He'd texted and emailed nightly since her talk with Candee. Which, he'd admitted, had prompted his return.

His emails were humorous and engaging, often describing a nonsensical situation occurring at work—a customer demanding a slice of huckleberry pie, although his bakery clearly sold only muffins and cupcakes and croissants, or an experimental batch of seaweed muffins everyone refused to eat.

We try to sell healthy selections once in a while, he'd joked.

What did you do with all those wholesome muffins? she'd asked.

I gave them to my skinny employees. Along with the remaining seaweed.

Oftentimes, his solutions to her work-related questions were exceptional. And when she uploaded photos of the daily progress to share with him, he replied instantly. Nothing was too unsettling that Rob couldn't solve with a clever, sensible remedy.

Each evening, when she was too exhausted to decide on another scone recipe or the installation of a gas versus a wood-burning fireplace, she looked forward to the end of her workday. She could finally climb the stairs to her apartment, open her laptop, and eagerly read his email.

When worries about money kept her awake at night, Rob would message her as soon as she logged onto her computer, as if he'd waited up for her. Sometimes, his messages were flirtatious. The actuality that he was eight hundred miles away made their exchanges feel safe and risk-free, and she enjoyed the playful bantering.

"The place looks better in person than in your photos," Rob said as she plucked up the bouquet and they stepped inside. He beamed his approval, sniffing the cedar-scented air and indicating the blazing logs in the stone-faced fireplace. "You decided on wood instead of gas after all."

"Aye." She went to the sink, retrieved a crystal vase, and arranged the flowers. "It's more work, but wood-burning is more authentic. And Teddy's hard-working crew deserves the credit, along with Candee's decorating expertise."

"I love these photographs." He stepped to a white-washed wall and surveyed the black and white photos of the old diner.

"I chose to pay homage to the diner's legacy. This place is riddled in history and was originally named Betty's Diner."

She'd set a table in Victorian style, complete with an Irish lace tablecloth, bone china cups, and polished silver. She set the vase of flowers in the center.

"Do you like the ambience?" she asked, following his reaction.

"Very, very much." He lifted back a pale-blue wool Oriental rug. "The wide plank oak floors are gleaming and rustic, which was the effect you were going for, right?"

"Absolutely." She tipped up her chin. "The crystal chandeliers will be hung tomorrow. And the paintings depict Ireland's landscapes. I placed them on the wall opposite the photographs, highlighting the old and the new, and two different cultures." She indicated a particularly poignant watercolor of a stone castle atop a hill, the rugged coastline and sea beyond. "I borrowed this concept from Danny Brady. Irish murals grace the walls in The Ground Café."

Rob came beside her. "Kathleen, you are a treasure." His sincere smile melted her heart. He bent his head and kissed her temple, then brushed a butterfly kiss on her lips. Joy surged through her that had nothing to do with his compliment. She couldn't believe this delightful man was interested in her.

And he was. It showed in his avid gaze, his steady eye contact and how he engaged her in endless chats.

"Would you prefer high tea or afternoon tea?" she asked.

"What's the difference?"

She glanced at her wristwatch. "It's around four, so afternoon tea is better."

"Again, what's the difference?"

"Mostly the seating. Afternoon tea is best experienced on low parlor chairs. If it's a high-backed chair, then it's high tea."

"Easy facts to remember," he said. "So these are low chairs."

"Correct."

"Is there a story behind high and low tea you can place on your menus?"

"I'll give you the abridged edition if you're interested."

"If it concerns you, I'm very interested."

"Well, teatime is a British tradition." She steepled her fingers. "Customarily, tea, scones, cakes and sandwiches were served in the nineteenth century. Teatime filled the gap between lunch and dinner, which was usually eaten around eight o'clock."

"I eat muffins every day at four. Should I call my snacks teatime?"

"If you'd like." She chuckled. "Nowadays, obviously, routines have changed. However, teatime is still observed as a civilized tradition. More important, it brings friends and family together and allows everyone the chance to slow down."

His eyes crinkled into a smile. "I'm more than ready to slow down."

Aye, she reasoned, noting the low crease in his forehead. Despite his smile, he looked as exhausted as she felt.

She whisked a glance at a log dropping in the fireplace. The wood sparked and crackled. Knowing his gaze was on her, she donned her prettiest beam. "So, shall we enjoy afternoon tea?"

"Sure. I think."

She laughed out loud at his wary expression. "You think?"

"Mind briefing me on what afternoon tea entails? I understand the four o'clock part, but is this another no thank you three times discussion?"

"We've done all that." She gestured for him to sit in a flowered parlor chair at the intimate table set for two.

He didn't.

Instead, he pulled out a chair for her before claiming his own. He was a gentleman in numerous ways, opening doors for her, never sitting if she was standing. Always, he was respectful and polite.

She poured the hot tea, which she'd prepared ahead. Gold flatware glinted by the light of tea candles, and metallic gold linen napkins folded in the shape of a crown sat on bone-china plates, the plates so translucent as to be almost see-through. A tiered platter was set with scones, finger sandwiches, clotted cream, and strawberry preserves.

"Is your tea dark enough?" she inquired.

He made a show of examining the brew in his gold-rimmed cup. "Strong enough to trot a mouse in."

"Here, here." She chuckled. "You're learning the Irish sayings quickly."

They bowed their heads and prayed a blessing. When they finished, she presented turkey sandwiches covered in cranberry jelly from the platter.

"I could get used to this," he laughed, taking a bite of a cucumber finger sandwich spread with herbed cream. "How did you make the cream?" he asked.

"It's not difficult. I'll lend you the recipe."

He settled in, slid his teacup closer, and supported his elbows on the table. Tea sloshed over the rim of his cup. "Kathleen, you've made the entire process look easy. You're going to open without a hitch."

The table wobbled, the legs uneven. And with that, the exquisite settings, hot tea, sandwiches, and flower-filled vase clattered to the floor.

Kathleen caught her teacup between her palms, although the brew spilled across her pinstriped blouse, leaving behind a splotchy wet stain. She dabbed at her shirt, her fingertips catching the droplets.

"Aye," she echoed, perching on the edge of her chair. "I'll be opening without a hitch."

CHAPTER EIGHT

To his customers and everyone in Miami who presumed to know him, Rob's bakeries were the epitome of success. To Rob, his bakeries were fast becoming a weight too heavy to carry on his broad shoulders.

And he was seriously considering selling everything.

More and more, Miami had become a place he sought to escape. He was tired of setting aside his personal life for an ever-elusive joy, no matter the vast amount of wealth and accolades he'd accumulated.

He craved laughter and companionship with people he enjoyed.

With Kathleen.

However, he also wanted to make certain their bond was more than a casual exchange between two businesspeople.

The following afternoon, he sat in the back room of Kathleen's teahouse with his cell-phone on speaker. George, his manager, was working in the Miami office, and he'd asked David, the newbie, to be his messenger and relay the bad news to Rob.

Butter prices had substantially risen and were up by 75 percent.

"Tell George to shop around," Rob told David.

"He has, Mr. Rob," David said. "All the local vendors and bulk supply stores have increased their prices."

"Their timing is perfect for the spring baking season. That is, perfect for them," Rob said sardonically. "I'll recalculate our muffin prices so we can stay within profit margins."

"Not possible, sir, unless you're planning to charge five dollars per muffin," David said. "We're currently selling at two dollars apiece."

"And losing money," Rob pointed out. "Although no customer will buy a five-dollar muffin, no matter how marvelous."

"Correct, sir."

"I'm proud of my products. However, I'm not in business to give them away." Impatience thickened Rob's tone. "Tell him."

"Yes, sir." David muffled the phone, and returned a minute later. "George said he's well aware of that, sir."

Heaving a sigh, Rob tipped his head against the back of the chair.

"Rob?" After a light tap on the door, Kathleen's voice floated through the room. "Oh, sorry." She put a hand to her mouth in apology. "I didn't realize you were still on the phone."

The afternoon sun shone through the window, splashing her cheeks with a hint of color. The past three days, she'd worked nonstop from early morning to late evening. Between Teddy's crew and a constant stream of suppliers, organized commotion heralded each new day. Rob had appeared each morning at daybreak, rolled up his sleeves, and worked alongside her.

He smiled at her, stood, and held up an index finger to let her know he was finishing the call.

"Text me later with a better update," he said to David. "Or we'll be churning our own butter."

"No worries. We'll need a cow, though, sir."

Rob stared at his cell-phone in stunned disbelief.

Apparently waiting for a response, David stacked on more assurances. "Actually ... we'll probably need two cows, sir."

Frustration reduced Rob's response to a groan. When he did speak, he kept his tone purposefully calm. "Thanks for the helpful tip, David. Goodbye for now." He clicked his phone shut and tossed it across the table.

Kathleen's lips twitched, a twinkle in her sparkling eyes. "You're in the business of buying cows now, are you? I'll take a half dozen. I heard Candee and Teddy own a pasture."

He laughed heartily. With her, every minute was like being in the middle of a splendid dream. She had an aura of exhilaration, a freshness sparking something inside him. Most important, she let him forget his cares, at least for a while.

Strawberry-blond tendrils had worked loose from her high ponytail, which she'd tied back with a teal satin ribbon. She wore a stretchy-knit yellow dress with a pretty V-neckline and tan loafers.

He'd dated beautiful women in his lifetime. No one compared to Kathleen. Perhaps it was her porcelain complexion, or the figure-hugging dress showing off her curves, or her shiny hair glinting in the sunlight. Perhaps it was because, besides being downright striking, she was chic and confident.

And yet she had never married. What was going on in Ireland? Were all the men blind?

Grinning, he placed his hand on his heart. "Kathleen, have I told you you're gorgeous? I liked the jeans you wore yesterday, but the dress—"

"Aye, you have, and often." She laughed. "And I've thanked you for your kindness each and every time."

"You're very welcome." He stepped closer and tucked a silky tendril behind her ear, his fingers brushing across her high cheekbone. "I applaud your conviction to follow your dreams. You're a determined, sharp-witted businessperson."

She rubbed her palm against the door which had been sanded and stained to a satiny oak finish. "Same as you, aye?"

"Yes, and I don't know if that's a good thing or a bad thing."

"What do you mean?"

"When you're focused on victory at all costs, it's easy to forget the important things in life."

A quiet smile, not quite reaching her eyes, lit her fine-boned face.

He was extremely attracted to her and wondered if it was a good idea to work so closely. He was caught up in her. She was caught up in her business.

He knew the feeling. He'd lived that way most of his adult life. And if he continued analyzing their situation, the fifteen-year difference between them would clutter things up even more.

She extended her hands, apparently unaware of his thoughts. "I hope butter hasn't risen significantly in the Carolinas," she said.

He took her small hands in his. "I'll check in the morning." He perused her flawless figure before his gaze slid to her face. "In the meantime, there's something else we can do besides churn butter."

"What?" She didn't seem to notice the telltale huskiness in his tone.

He pulled her near and pressed a kiss on her hair, her temple, her cheeks.

"Rob ..." She gazed up at him and licked her lips. "Maybe we should—"

He swallowed hard. "Kiss?" He framed her face in his hands, stared at her mouth and bent his head.

From the entrance, a crewman's voice called out. The workers were leaving.

Immediately, she stepped back. "I should see them out."

"Why? They can find their way through the front door. They've worked every day since I've been here."

"Aye, but—"

"Kathleen, are you comfortable with us ... with me ..." Wow, did he ever sound desperate. Quickly, he closed his mouth before he revealed something he'd regret.

"Surely you understand I didn't come to America to find a man."

"And surely you understand there's a magnetism drawing us together."

"Your businesses will be calling you back soon enough, so we shouldn't get too attached to each other."

He tried his most charming grin. "Why not?"

"It's like giving biscuits to a bear."

There went her Irish slang, and he had no notion of what she was talking about. "Meaning?"

"Our being together is a waste of time. Look at what I've undertaken. I can't manage anything more."

He got it. He'd take it slow. She had mountains of tasks, and it was too soon for a commitment.

"Will you take a wee peek at the kitchen in my apartment?" she asked, her tone shifting to businesslike. "The crewmen have enough to complete down here, and one of my shelves needs an adjustment."

"I'm not a carpenter."

"It isn't a complicated job." She led him through the rooms, separated by brick archways, and paused by the staircase. "If you fix the shelf, I'll best the deal with a warm bowl of colcannon."

At his puzzled expression, she clarified, "Mashed potatoes mixed with kale, scallions, milk and butter. And I'll fry you a pan of sausages on the side."

"Free labor for free food," he said. "How can I refuse when I'm ravenous?"

He was ravenous all right. He wanted to hold her, glide his fingers through her strawberry-blond hair, spend hours chatting with her. Kissing her.

As he accompanied her up the creaky wooden stairs, she remarked, "My father never owned anything he couldn't fix."

Rob grimaced. Aware he didn't immediately respond, and likewise aware she was waiting, he contemplated telling her the truth. He'd never been handy with tools, and if she evaluated a man by his hammer wielding abilities, he'd fail miserably.

"That's the way with most men, isn't it?" she added.

Real men fix things. He visualized the slogan—resembling a television commercial.

The tension in his shoulders tightened with each ascending step. He hoped she wouldn't judge him for not being able to hang cabinets or install crown molding, because his reply would be *I can't.* His affluent parents had deemed carpentry beneath them, and encouraged Rob to perform well in school and play sports.

So he had, excelling at both.

And his father had continued to beat him. They'd kept it hidden, presenting a fake façade to their community. Despite the proper upbringing in the proper home, there was no love; only disinterest, indifference, and cruelty. However, they'd filled their home with material possessions, and Rob never lacked the latest tech toy.

After his father had broken Rob's nose once, he'd whipped

out his checkbook and bought Rob a Camaro for his sixteenth birthday.

"I can fix this," his father had said, as if a new Camaro could fix a broken nose.

It had come as no surprise his parents didn't approve of his baking career. Although he became a prosperous businessperson, they'd dismissed his achievements.

And now they were gone. A few years earlier, they'd died within months of each other, both from lung cancer. Rob was an only child, and had tried to accept the fact he had failed them, but he never did.

Ten minutes later, he found himself crouched beneath a loose corner shelf in Kathleen's kitchen.

"Can you hand me a hammer, Kathleen?" he asked with a nail held between his teeth.

"Aye," she obliged.

He pinched a second nail between his thumb and index finger, lined the nails up and gave them several sharp whacks. Two nails hammered at once seemed more efficient. Thankfully, she seemed blissfully unaware of his many misses as he attempted to drive the nails into the board and kept slamming his thumb instead. He held in his colorful curses and tried again. Finally, on the fifth attempt, he succeeded.

He stood and wiped wood particles from his jeans. "All set."

There it was. The shelf was secure. Now he could swing a hammer like any of the burly men on Teddy's construction crew.

Her gracious smile filled with appreciation. "What would I do without all this help?"

He prayed she'd narrow her selection down to one helpful person: him. She simply couldn't accomplish this project without *him*.

She slipped off her loafers. "I have something special for us!"

"A wee bit of whiskey?" He peered at her bare feet. "Will we be stomping the whiskey like the Italians stomp grapes for wine?"

"I don't drink," she reminded, skipping to a CD player on the counter. "And what I planned is indeed better."

A lively jig sounded through the kitchen, played by the traditional Celtic instruments of a fiddle, flute, and tin whistle.

She held out her hands, positioning him to face her. "Dance with me, Rob."

He was almost as inept a dancer as he was a carpenter, and he primed the argument on his tongue. "Kathleen, I'm a baker."

"You've repeated that a number of times. And so am I, but I also can dance." She dropped her hands to her sides, and he followed her lead.

"You're Irish," he said. "You've probably danced a jig your entire life."

She wasn't listening. "First, assume the stance." She bounced with the beat, shoulders back and head held high.

He tried to imitate her and carry out her instructions—cross your feet, point your right toe, do a hop, hop back, and lead with your left.

"Leave it to you Irish to make your dance as complicated as drinking tea," he groaned.

She laughed. "Execute the reel straightaway." She whirled him around in a circle, sending her knit dress flying up and exposing shapely bare legs.

He pulled a handkerchief from his pocket to wipe the sweat from his forehead. He was dizzy, he was breathless. And he was laughing with an abandonment he hadn't felt since he was little.

She giggled, her deep dimples showing. As the jig ended, she collapsed against him. Tears of laughter streamed down her flushed cheeks. "Not so difficult, aye? You danced grand."

"And you're amazing." He caught her tears with his knuckles. In his arms, she was soft and light and he tightened his grip. He was charmed and totally besotted, and he couldn't recall ever being as in love with a woman.

Whoa. Hold that thought.

"I'll teach you the Irish jig whenever you'd like," she was saying. "There're more steps."

"Uh-huh, I'm sure there's a whole book full. I'll put jigs on a back burner for now, but you're an admirable instructor," he said. "And your cooking—"

"Oh, that reminds me." She tore away. "I'll warm the colcannon. That's part of our deal."

"How about a tour first? I spend most of my life in a kitchen."

She tapped a hand to her forehead. "I forgot you haven't seen the rest of my apartment." A slow smile came across her face. "Although saying it's crying for a complete overhaul is an understatement. I've been too busy to entertain decorating ideas, and I admit it's not my strength."

Evidenced by her charming kitchen, she was more than capable. She obviously set high standards for herself.

They wandered through the half-empty rooms—bathroom, hallway, and bedroom. The bare walls were devoid of mementos—no pictures, no window treatments save for shades, no framed photographs of loved ones. The carpet was bland and tattered, the white paint peeling from the ceiling. A chipped farmhouse stool stood as a table beside a worn plaid couch, a knitted blue blanket draped over an end chair. In the corner, wind whistled through cracks in the walls.

Where were her personal belongings? He considered

asking, but didn't. She'd admitted to missing Ireland. Possibly she was hesitant to set down permanent roots in America.

Suppose she decided to leave? He captured the troublesome thought and kept it in the forefront of his mind.

"Lovely," he crooned politely as they reentered the kitchen.

"You're too kind." She removed the mashed potato mixture from the refrigerator and transferred it to a pan on the stove.

He grabbed plates and silverware and set the table before coming to stand beside her. "And you work too hard."

"Not any harder than you. Besides—"

"Therefore, I declare tomorrow afternoon a sightseeing holiday."

"Rob, I can't possibly take off an afternoon. Anyway, I'll be knackered."

He quirked an eyebrow.

"Tired. I'll be tired," she said.

"You'll be more productive afterward. What's more, this town is the size of a postage stamp."

"We'll stay in town?"

"For the most part."

She frowned, crunching her delicate eyebrows together. "What's that supposed to mean?"

"It means I plan to show you something first. Then we'll eat dinner at a farm-to-table restaurant that's drawing glowing reviews. Aren't you interested in your local competition?"

"I'm running a teahouse."

"They serve food. You'll be serving food. Maybe new recipe ideas will inspire you."

Ever the entrepreneur, her face lit up. "I guess I can quit at four o'clock."

"Make it three. Where we're going will require a few

hours of daylight." He glanced down at her smoky eyes, placed a kiss on her lips, and added a wink.

"Ooh. Sounds mysterious. We're not staying in Roses, then?"

He shrugged. "There's a surprise first."

"I don't usually like surprises. Is this a good surprise?"

"It's a fun surprise," he corrected. "And one I'd like your opinion on."

She gave the colcannon a quick stir, then twisted. "Alright, then. Brilliant."

He smiled. The main thing was that they were going to enjoy an afternoon outside of work. And, by doing so, he'd show her why she should settle in Roses for good.

CHAPTER NINE

The following afternoon, Kathleen hummed "Molly Malone", a favorite tune, as Rob pulled up in his candy-red rental car. The afternoon was balmy, foreshadowing the pleasant weather to come.

They'd stopped working at two o'clock after the power had unexpectedly shut off, leaving the crewmen and teahouse in darkness. Fortunately, the electric company had responded and quickly restored power, giving her the opportunity for a hot shower.

She'd taken care with her appearance, dressing in a royal-blue cotton dress with a flared skirt. She paired the dress with brown leather ankle boots and dark tights, topping the outfit with a twill jacket in a light pink print. She'd scrubbed, blow dried, and brushed her long hair until it crackled and shone. Leaving it to lie in loose ringlets around her shoulders, she donned a jaunty straw hat and pinned it in place.

She called out a cheerful greeting as Rob got out of the car. He was at her door before she'd taken a step.

"My beautiful Kathleen." He kissed her warmly on the lips. "Good to see you again."

"You just left my place an hour ago."

He smirked. "And I missed you the entire time." He opened the passenger door for her, and she settled into the plush leather seats.

"Where are we going?" she asked, buckling her seat belt.

He slid into the driver's seat and did the same. "It's a surprise, remember?"

"Rob, I've never liked surprises and—"

"I'll give you two hints." His teasing voice stilled her protests. "It's a town not far from here and it rhymes with toast."

"We're driving to the coast? But we're near the mountains."

Smiling, he pulled to the curb and turned to face her. "I'll give you another hint."

"Alright."

"Boo!"

She jumped, patting her heart. "What on earth? You scared me."

"Sorry." He planted a kiss on her temple, then eased the car back onto the road.

"So now it's presumed I know where we're going?"

He shrugged, an impish expression on his face. "I assumed my clues were useful."

She smiled. "A town rhyming with toast? Boo?" Her smile widened. "Those are clues? Even Sherlock Holmes would have given up."

Their gazes locked—his filled with mischief, hers with a hint of apprehension.

"The surprise is we're driving to Hollan Farms," he said.

"I've never heard of it."

"Teddy and I passed through when we drove from Asheville to Roses." Rob flicked on his blinker and followed a narrow two-lane road, the only traffic a bicycle rider and a lone scooter. "Hollan Farms is a ghost town."

Images of American cowboys and deserted gold rush cities came to mind. "Here? In the Southeast?"

"Technically, a few inhabitants still live there. Sit back and enjoy the ride." He switched on the radio, and James Taylor sang about seeing fire and rain.

They arrived a half hour later, and Rob parked in a graveled car park at the edge of town. Before she could open the door and reach for her straw clutch handbag, he came around and assisted her.

She linked her hand through his arm, their pleasant banter and discerning observations progressing with each step.

"There's a general belief that ghost towns are creepy and haunted," he said. "From my research, this town is none of these."

"Except it does looks abandoned." She pointed to a string of empty storefronts. "It doesn't take a genius to realize no one has lived here for a while."

"Yes, there's that."

Her cheeks warmed as he regarded her, his gaze moving to her lips before he took her in his arms and kissed her.

She was with him far too often. He was the picture of who and what she'd intended to avoid—a good-looking man sharing precious, remarkable moments with her.

Risky, risky, risky. If she continued along this path, eventually her heart would be broken.

But this was Rob, and he was different.

Aye. Different all right. He was too appealing, too perceptive, too much of a distraction.

Too much of an *attraction.*

A light breeze caused her straw hat to flap, and she placed one hand on top of her head to steady it. Trees on every street corner blossomed, sending tiny white petals floating through the air.

As they wound through a forsaken alleyway, Rob seemed to take in every element of the buildings—the worn scalloped awning on the supermarket, abandoned café tables outside a bistro, an ornamental stone fountain. She imagined water bursting from the basin, children playing around it, street vendors selling bunches of flowers and delectable coffee and desserts.

"This was a boomtown, a resort boasting a healing hot spring, luxurious spa, and top-rate restaurants," Rob said. "The town went belly up because of the economic downturn a few years ago. Sadly, the anticipated clientele—middle America—could no longer afford spa vacations."

She slowed to peer through a dusty café window. Chairs and tables were arranged in the middle of the floor, menus stacked by the receptionist's booth as if frozen in time.

"And the hot spring?" she inquired.

"What about it?"

"Where is it?"

"It still runs through the center of town."

The sky changed to a dove gray, and the sun disappeared. A minute later, a heavy rain shower caught her sleeves with drops of water.

"Hold on to your hat," Rob joked. He grabbed her hand and led her on a race through the streets.

"This happens in Ireland constantly," she said, winded and laughing. "One minute it's sunny, the next, rain is bucketing down."

They ducked beneath the canopied entrance of a once impressive hotel, the windows reflecting a marbled tile entryway and carpet at least ten years old.

"It storms and rains on many hot afternoons in Miami too," Rob said.

Water dripped from the brim of her hat, a puddle forming at their feet. "Except Ireland's weather is a wee bit cooler than Miami, to be sure."

"You think?"

"I know for certain." Her hand was still clasped in his warm one. This close, with his warm blue eyes framed by thick brows and his ever-present smile, he exuded self-assurance. Not arrogant the way some men she'd dated carried themselves, more interested in their lives than anything she had to say.

As she gazed up at Rob, she noticed his nose had been broken at least once. Tenderly, she ran her finger across the bridge. "What happened?" she asked softly.

"He liked whiskey and bourbon and cigarettes."

"Who?"

"My father." Rob was silent for several beats. "The combination was frightening when he was angry."

"Your father." She mulled the two words in her mind. Rob rarely spoke about his family or his past. "Did he ... break your nose?"

"Yes."

"So, he beat you?"

"Often."

"Oh, Rob." What could she say? She knew from Clara's brother, Seamus, how alcohol twisted a person's life into a roller-coaster, the ups and downs catching loved ones in a virtual whirlwind of emotions. Inevitably, wreckage and despair followed.

"It happened years ago. Decades, literally." Rob spoke so softly she wasn't sure she heard him. She thought he dabbed at his eyes.

She pictured him as a small boy, chubby, sweet-faced, an infectious beam in his deep-set eyes. "It's alright," she finally said.

"What I remember most is the smell of my father's whiskey and cigarette breath, and the sight of him asleep at the oak desk in his study, an empty liquor bottle lying beside him. I tried to please him, I really did."

The neediness in Rob's voice warmed a secret place in her heart. Perhaps that was why he'd tried so hard all these years to succeed—in his effort to satisfy parents who didn't care. He was a pleaser, thinking of everyone except himself.

"I'm sorry." Something inside prompted her to squeeze his hand and offer reassurance. "The future is what matters."

They stood quiet, the steady rain beating down on the hotel's canopy. He stared at her so long a shiver coursed through her. He trusted her enough to share his heart-breaking memories.

Truly, he cared about her.

And she, in turn, cared about him. Trusted him.

More than cared. More than trusted. She was falling in love with him.

No. Not here. Not now.

Then where, exactly? And when? All she needed to do was gaze at him. The confirmation stood directly in front of her—with his every intention, and devotion shining from his brilliant blue eyes. Somehow, in the madness of two different worlds, they'd found each other.

Knowing her rain-dampened cheeks were a hot pink, she broke the spell and spun to peer through the hotel's grimy window. She tented her hands and read the scrawled sign posted in the lobby. "We are open to patrons during the summer months."

"Wow," Rob said. "Business is booming."

She laughed and pivoted. "For who, exactly?"

"I don't know. It might be an old sign."

"Didn't you say a handful of people still live in Hollan Farms?"

"Yes, but they wouldn't stay at the hotel."

"So, where are they?"

He shrugged. Gently, he wiped rain droplets off her chin. "They're probably in Asheville for the day."

"The entire population?"

"The entire population of ten."

The rain stopped as suddenly as it had started. He kept hold of her hand as they continued their exploration, answering her speculative questions with speculative answers. Eventually, they crossed a rickety wooden bridge.

The famed babbling hot spring nestled beside budding trees and shrubs, and Kathleen caught her breath at the exquisite sight. With mountain views in the distance, the scene could have been a page removed from a travel brochure advertising tranquility.

"Beautiful," she murmured. "Like a fairy-tale reproduction of what real life should be."

"Zen."

At her raised eyebrows, he explained, "Zen is Japanese slang for serenity."

She gazed upward and sighed. White, wispy clouds floated above, drifting leisurely. No rush for the clouds. Nature was never in a hurry. If only she could harness that same inner peace.

Directly opposite the sun, a muted band of colors formed an arc. "Look, Rob." She pointed. "A rainbow!"

"I'll snap a photo."

"Quick, before it disappears."

He pulled his cell-phone from his pocket, stepped beside her, and snapped a selfie of them framed by the rainbow.

She was too enchanted by this fascinating town to object.

"You're prettier than any rainbow." Rob hung his arm around her shoulders. "But I can delete the photo if—"

"No, of course not." She wanted to relish the growing

attraction between them, to spend every precious minute with him. Everything about him was appealing—each shared glance, the feel of his callused hand around hers, his agreeable, mellow nature.

She peered at the sky. Already, the rainbow was fading. A homesickness she hadn't felt in a while enveloped her.

"Are you okay?" he asked.

"I'm fine." She brushed her fingers across her eyes. "Oftentimes, the rainbows in Ireland are brilliant."

"Rainbows are brilliant in America too, Kathleen. And Roses is your new home."

Here. With me.

The words dangled between them.

"Do you desire a soak, my lady?" he asked when they reached the edge of the hot spring. "You know, all those healing powers ..."

"I didn't bring my swimsuit," she joked.

"A pity." He moved behind her and wrapped his hands around her waist, nuzzling her neck. She turned, considering, then stood on her tiptoes and kissed him.

He drew an inward breath and folded her in his arms. She wrapped her hands around his nape.

This was decisive.

She was done worrying about dating, or relationships, or whether this was the right time. Because here was Rob, a man she trusted. She loved the way his lips were firm, yet tender and enticing. He was so good to her, polite, calm, respectful.

When the kiss ended, he whispered, "You have no idea how often I think about you."

Likewise. He was in her thoughts every minute.

He beckoned her to dip her hands into the water with him.

"I read that famous actors and actresses who visited here often immersed themselves in the healing waters," he said.

Kathleen splashed water on her face. "Whether the spring is healing or not, this town is delightful."

"I agree." He looked around, pensive, deliberating. "And it's for sale."

"What is?" She aimed her gaze across the street. "The hotel?"

"The town."

Playfully, she swatted him. "A town can't be for sale."

"Sure it can."

The whole town was for sale.

And Rob had a gleam in his eyes she instantly recognized. Once an entrepreneur, always an entrepreneur.

"How much?" she asked.

"I've done some investigating. Plus, Candee's a real estate agent, which is helpful."

"How much?" she repeated.

"Several million dollars."

He might as well have stated several trillion dollars; the amount was so removed from her stratosphere.

"Rob, surely you're not thinking of buying a ... town."

He chuckled. "Teddy and Candee voiced the same reservation."

"What about your bakeries?"

"I'm putting them up for sale. I'm retiring."

She touched a hand to her parted lips. "You'd sell Rob's Marvelous Muffins?"

"I'll keep the name and unload the buildings, retail spaces and my condo. I'll start the paperwork when I fly to Miami."

"Is this wise? You've established a wonderful reputation. What about your recipes, your customer base—"

His jaw set. "All too much work."

"Compared to renovating a town?" She couldn't find a coherent sentence to sputter. "Along with the actual price, it'll take several more millions to fix all the buildings."

"True." Lazily, he stroked a stray ringlet falling across her shoulder.

She stepped back. "Isn't that a lot of money?"

"Yes. However, Hollan Farms has one thing Miami lacks."

His words caught, and she looked up at him. The entire afternoon had followed its own course. And in his explanation, she recognized a deep emotion. Commitment.

"Healing spring water?" she half teased.

"Guess again."

"Rob, I ..." She'd forgotten her guesses, anyway. When she was with him, she forgot all her troubles.

She knew he watched her, so she ventured, "The town offers dilapidated cafés just waiting for your marvelous muffins?"

"Nope."

"What could Hollan Farms possibly offer that isn't in Miami?"

"You." He brought her into his arms, bent his head, and thoroughly kissed her. "I'm planning to move to Roses permanently."

When their tour of the town ended, the sun hung low in the sky, the beginnings of a sunset casting vivid purple and orange hues that shadowed the derelict buildings. By the time they arrived at the farm-to-table restaurant, stars blanketed a clear night sky.

Rob's admission that he would sell all he'd built in order to be close to her had successfully breached the last of her defenses. Here she'd assumed the wall barricading her heart had been honed to perfection and nothing could penetrate it. And it had been so, until she'd met this honest, mature gentleman. Until the impossible had occurred.

She'd fallen for him, and there was no turning back.

"Are you hungry?" he inquired.

"I'm starving, actually."

"Next time we go to the hot spring, we'll pack a picnic."

Next time. A promise of shared experiences to come. Celebrations.

Seeing the restaurant's parking lot packed with cars, she remarked, "We may not be eating here tonight."

"I made reservations," he said.

His cell-phone pinged. He darted a glance at the caller ID and scowled. "Sorry, Kathleen, I need to take this. One of my managers—"

She drew in a breath before a sharp retort rolled from her tongue. *Rob,* she wanted to say. *Must your business always come first?*

After a clipped exchange, Rob ended the call.

Scents of smoked bacon and fresh-baked rolls wafted from the doorway as they ascended the restaurant's stairs. Inside, the walls were decorated in cherry-wood paneling. Candlelight and a pianist playing soft background music—well-known Broadway show tunes—completed the understated elegance.

As Rob hung her jacket, Kathleen removed her floppy hat and peered at her outfit, grateful she'd worn a dress.

When they were seated, a black-clad waiter brought menus, explaining the food was fresh and locally sourced, while he poured glasses of sparkling water.

She enjoyed an exquisite meal of a seared chicken breast served on a bed of roasted mushrooms and cherry tomatoes, while Rob opted for the grilled beef tenderloin with spinach and spaghetti squash.

For dessert, she ordered black coffee and a cherry fruit cobbler. She forked a piece of the crust and chewed discerningly.

"How is it?" Rob asked. He'd ordered bread pudding filled with frozen grapes, and raisin rum ice cream on the side.

She placed the fork near her plate and patted her lips with the linen napkin. "Surprisingly mediocre. Yours?"

"The same." He toyed with the pudding, then scooped up a spoonful of ice cream. "Odd, because dinner was delicious. I wonder if they outsource their desserts because I know a certain woman who bakes a heavenly brown bread." A not-so-secret smile appeared on his lips.

Chuckling, she shook her head. "I have enough on my plate baking bread and scones for my patrons-to-be. What about you?"

"I'm retiring, remember?"

Sure, by buying and restoring a ghost town boasting a hot spring, grocery store, hotel, and who knew what else.

As she sipped her coffee, she felt an unexplainable surge of pride for his tenaciousness. Although he'd told her he didn't have a bit of Irish blood in him—his surname, Taylor, being French and Scottish—he was as sharp-witted as any Irishman.

"What's the finest dessert you've ever tasted?" she asked.

In the softness of candlelight, his face appeared younger. He looked rested and happy. "Your brown bread."

She smiled over the rim of her cup. "No, really."

"There's a mom-and-pop restaurant near Asheville. I dined there with Teddy a while back, and the owners specialize in homemade apple cobblers topped with a flaky crust. I'll take you there some time." He leaned in. "What about you?"

"Ah, well, in Ireland, any coffee shop or café will likely serve desserts prepared in-house."

"I'd like to visit Ireland someday," he said quietly.

Don't go there, she thought. A small part of her

demanded she stay on track—launching an up-and-coming teahouse in America. That meant no distractions.

But then, she'd already made her decision. With Rob, her world had changed. They could enjoy America and Ireland together, as a team, as a couple, as two people devoted to each other.

She sat back in the tufted chair, moving in time to the pianist's rendition of the upbeat "I Could Have Danced All Night" from *My Fair Lady*.

She tilted back her head, her smile lighthearted. "It would be an honor to show you my country, Rob."

"I can't wait."

She inhaled, treasuring the moment. She'd made the correct choice coming to Roses, and she wanted Rob in her life.

The way he smiled back at her told her everything. It warmed her weary heart, and there was no mistaking the love in his expression.

CHAPTER TEN

"I'll depart for Miami tomorrow," Rob told Kathleen a few days after they'd dined at the farm-to-table restaurant. They stood on the front porch of her teahouse on a brisk day in early March. A sharp breeze ruffled the burgundy striped awning that had recently been installed.

She swallowed and avoided his gaze. "Seven days seems like forever."

"I'm merely a few hours away by plane. In the meantime, I have a gift so you won't forget me." He withdrew a silver-foil-wrapped box from his sport jacket and handed it to her.

Solemnly, he watched her open a black velvet box and snap open the lid. Inside was a Victorian heart-shaped skeleton key locket on a cable chain, plated in twenty-four carat gold.

"Thank you," she said. "It's beautiful."

"For a beautiful woman." He secured the chain around her neck. "My Irish queen, you hold the key to my heart. Always remember that."

She laughed. "Fit for a queen, aye?"

"Yes." He nodded. "Open the locket."

She popped the magnetic closure, and all laughter vanished from her face. She studied the miniature photo tucked inside—the one he'd taken of them at Hollan Farms with the stunning rainbow in the background.

"Turn the locket over," he instructed.

On the back was inscribed: 1-800-IRELAND.

Tears welled in her eyes. "Thank you," she said again.

"I hope you will always think of me when you wear it."

"Every day."

"That's what I like to hear." He embraced her in a loving hold. Against her cheek, his chest was warm and comforting, his heartbeat steady and sure. "I'll return well before your grand opening. I promise, and I never go back on my word."

He was considerate and compassionate, intuitive to her feelings.

She acknowledged his promise, although tears burned. "I'll miss you," she said.

"Not as much as I'll miss you."

She declined his pocket handkerchief that he offered, her thoughts scattering.

When he was near, she felt treasured. Now these crucial hours leading up to March 17 would continue without him.

Well, she'd steel her shoulders and deal with it. He had a business to run. So did she. Furthermore, she was a resourceful entrepreneur. Rob had told her so himself.

He pressed a kiss on her lips. "I'll call as soon as I land in Miami." His gaze flicked to the crewmen busily making adjustments to the wood floor in one of the dining rooms. "Teddy, Candee, Keiran, and Desiree are all around, so you won't be alone."

Despite his assurances, a moment of sadness went through her, just long enough to cause her chest to ache. She was truly alone now.

Woodenly, she nodded. "Aye."

And with that, the next day he was gone.

As the week passed, she enlisted Teddy's crew as taste testers while she perfected scones and breads. Happily, they obliged.

Candee designed a high-quality menu, and aprons were ordered to match Kathleen's teahouse logo. At the last minute, the crewmen erected a pergola to the outside seating area, where bottled water, tea, and fruit juices would be sold.

Kathleen stationed a NOW HIRING sign near the entrance of the teahouse, and several applicants immediately responded. Interviewing the bright-faced candidates left her invigorated and hopeful.

However, various decisions still loomed. Would customers prefer high tea or a more casual atmosphere? Parsnips in their soup or a traditional creamy broccoli? Spot-on decisions meant enthusiastic regulars, and she counted on Rob's daily answers to her texts.

As the days flew forward, two catastrophes occurred.

First, the large dough mixer wasn't expected to arrive on time after all.

Forcing herself to sound calm and unemotional, she phoned Rob.

"You have countertop hand mixers, right?" he asked.

"Aye, and a dough proofer and all the bakeware."

"Tell the two assistants you hired to use what's available. They're qualified, correct?"

"Which brings me to my second catastrophe." She could hardly voice the words. "One quit before she started because she said the start-up wage is too low. The other is in university and her work days are limited."

"Keep looking."

"I am. There may be a third applicant. Her name is Nancy, and she's enthusiastic and eager."

"How old is she?"

"Twenty-something. She's willing to work alongside me, doesn't mind long hours, and told me that my teahouse is unique and special."

"She's a keeper. People like that are hard to find, so train her well and take any spare minute to invest in her development. And don't forget to phone Keiran too. He's a block away."

"I did. O'Malley's is busier than ever and he can't spare anyone this close to St. Patrick's Day. Teddy has even bussed a few tables there to help Keiran out."

Rob blew out a sigh. "Unfortunately, being short-staffed is typical in this industry."

"Short-staffed is one thing. No staffed is another."

"Part-time employees aren't dependable. I'd refer a couple of mine, but with my stores for sale, everyone is in an upheaval. Many of my steady workers are seeking employment elsewhere."

"Didn't you assure them that their jobs were secure?"

"I tried, although new owners may bring aboard different people."

She paused. "Rob, can I ask you another question?"

"Certainly."

"Should I urge my customers to place their cell-phones in containers when they walk in? You know, to strengthen community, and encourage family conversations."

Through the phone, she heard a man speaking to Rob.

"Sorry Kathleen, it's David," Rob said.

"The cow guy?"

"Yes, and it's apparently urgent. Hang on." Rob muffled the phone. He addressed David's question, then came back on the line. "This place is like a zoo today. What were you saying?"

"Nothing." Kathleen's grip on her phone tightened. "I'll sort it out myself."

"Sorry," he said softly. "Once this place is sold, we'll be together."

When? Selling a huge commercial operation wouldn't be a matter of a few days. It would take weeks, maybe months. Maybe years.

She'd always found herself cheered after talking with Rob. However, her chin quivered as she felt her safeguards being swept aside. She relied on him, but he had enough on his hands without her constant barrage of questions. In the interim, she needed to trust her own business sense.

She inhaled deeply. "Do you remember Sean, my coworker at The Ground Café?"

"The guy who is supposedly interested in quitting his manager job in Ireland to lend you a hand in America?"

"I wouldn't put it that way, Rob," she corrected. "He isn't *supposedly* interested. He is interested and assured he won't accept a salary from me. Plus, he'd work full-time, so there's no dependability issue."

"You've discussed your last-minute problems with him, plus he'll work for free?" She could almost see Rob's eyes narrowing. "Why?"

"Because he's a friend." She bristled. "He's been nothing but supportive. He rang me again last night."

"And now he's phoning you as well as texting?"

"Only twice since you left. He's as experienced as you are."

"Your brogue is thickening, and you sound defensive, which is never a good sign." There was an inexplicable seriousness in Rob's tone, coupled with frustration. "And what did you tell Mr. Sean?"

"I told him I was handling things well on my own, although these days I'm thinking I can use his support. He's ringing me tomorrow morning."

"Sounds like you talk with this guy more than you talk with me."

"Don't be ridiculous. You and I chat every day. It's just that you're ... preoccupied." She couldn't remember the last time her conversation with Rob hadn't been interrupted at least once. And Sean was 100 percent available—and always sympathizing with her.

"Kathleen." Rob allowed the silence between them to go on for twice as long as she expected. "There's a lot involved here in Miami."

"I know." She squeezed her eyes shut. "And I should be more understanding."

He didn't say yes or no. Instead, he continued, "Several of my managers expressed interest in purchasing the entire business. That's heartening, because they've been with me for years and I trust them to maintain the quality. However, bank loan applications are time-consuming. Not to mention, my bakeries are all still running."

She needed him. Now. Didn't he realize that?

She shook her head. She was being selfish.

"I understand," she said quietly, although she heard the edge in her tone.

"Remember our ghost town. Our life together. Remember us."

Us.

The dovelike caress threading his words caused a delicious shiver up her spine.

"I'll remember." She gave a weary smile into the phone.

Hollan Farms. An empty shell of a town. Despite Rob's assurances, she felt similar to that town. Abandoned.

When her cell-phone rang at dawn, she recognized Sean's number on the caller ID. And when he asked if she required back-up relief, she answered with one word.

Aye.

He was capable. He was more than eager. And they'd worked closely before.

On a rain-soaked afternoon a couple days afterward, Sean appeared in Roses. His flights from Dublin to Asheville were brilliant, he assured. He'd hired an Uber for the final leg to Roses.

"You quit your job at The Ground Café?" Kathleen inquired as he met her under the front awning. Despite the heavy travel he looked well-rested, his olive-camouflage jacket and black pants washed and pressed.

"Aye. Howya." He placed his luggage on the stoop and grasped her in a fierce hug. "I'm tired of working for someone else."

"You'll work for me now."

He didn't answer. A shadow crossed his hard-lined face.

"Well, travel certainly agrees with you." She pondered her statement as she regarded him. "When I flew the transatlantic flight, it took me several days to recover from jet lag."

"Kathleen, I must confess." His gaze darted. "I landed in Boston last week."

"Boston?" With keen effort, she controlled her temper while drawing a slow breath. "I assumed you were in Ireland when you rang me."

"I figured I was off to America, anyway. A few days earlier didn't matter."

"And if I didn't accept your bid to help me?"

"Don't know." He waved his hands airily. His hazel eyes darkened. "I may have stayed in Boston, although I knew you'd come round eventually if I kept badgering."

Typical Sean. He'd always hassled big-hearted Danny Brady at The Ground Café, requesting weekends off or extended paid holidays until Danny agreed.

"You're obviously a pro at badgering," she said.

"I suppose I am."

She couldn't keep from staring at him. His medium-length dark hair had been styled into a kinky perm.

"Any comments?" He finger combed the curls. "A man perm is all the rage."

"It's ..." She stopped herself before saying *hysterically funny*, assuming he wouldn't appreciate the humor.

"Foxy?" he questioned.

"Aye, especially combined with your dark beard."

"*Go raibh míle maith agat.*"

Thanks a million. The familiar Irish words brought a rush of tears to her eyes.

"Can you recommend a place in town where I can rent a room?" he asked.

"There's a splendid bed-and-breakfast not far from here."

"And a pub with good craic?" He stepped too close, completely disregarding her personal space. "I'm definitely fond of parties."

She moved backward, remembering the times he'd reported to The Ground Cafe after going out on the lash and drinking. Although she'd often smelled alcohol on his breath, it hadn't seemed to affect his performance.

"If you're in search of lively banter," she pointed down the street, "Keiran O'Malley's pub is walking distance from here. Just don't drink on the days you're working."

"Wouldn't think of it."

"Do you remember Keiran's cousin William?" she asked.

"I do." His gaze leveled on her. "He won your affection and took you away from me."

"We're all just friends, Sean."

"I'd like us to be more than friends, Kathleen. Surely you must know that."

"Sean. No. Although I'm thankful for your support."

"Gotcha. Loud and clear." He raised his hands in feigned surrender. "As soon as I'm a wee bit settled, I'll visit Keiran's pub on my off days." His small hazel eyes left hers to regard the teahouse's green painted shingles. "Your place looks brilliant. The color reminds me of Ireland."

"Do you think so? Decorating isn't my forte, I just wanted an old European touch. Fortunately, my friend Candee guided me. I couldn't even choose curtains until she carried over several fabric swatches and I finally decided on a jewel-tone floral."

"Candee is your real estate agent?"

"Aye. Her husband, Teddy, is my contractor." Kathleen blew out a breath. "I'm trying hard to resist the impulse to text her every time there's a decorating problem."

"Luckily, here I am to solve everything." He picked up his luggage, and they stepped inside, the front bell tinkling to announce their arrival.

"Thanks for coming. You're an asset, Sean."

"It's because our Irish work ethic is first rate."

She grinned, turning her attention to the shelves teeming with tea. "Today I'm trying to decide how many loose-leaf blends to serve my customers."

"Less is better to keep the quality up."

"Sean, there are over 250 teas to choose from."

"From the looks of it, you've bought them all." He planted his hands on his bony hips. "Stick with a basic selection of twelve."

"I planned a high tea every day at four o'clock. Is that too much?"

"Roses is a little-bitty town," he said. "Compromise and serve high tea on weekends only. You'll end up failing if you overextend yourself."

"You're right," she said.

His boots clicked across the wood floors, and she glided

her hand over a lavish tea service she'd polished until the silver gleamed. "I can't believe you flew such a long way for me."

"My pleasure." Lightly, he brushed a curl coming loose from her pony tail in much the same way when they'd worked double shifts together and were exhausted at the end of the day. "You remember I'm the adventurous sort. Like you."

She also remembered he used to point that out a lot. *Spirited go-getters intent on success,* he'd say. Somehow, the words didn't sound as flattering as they once did.

In the ensuing days, Sean inched his way into becoming an integral part of every decision, from improving providers' terms to mounting a decorative box next to each table for cell-phones.

He was shrewd, often voicing her objectives before she did, or latching on to an idea and expanding it. He repeatedly pointed out that her concepts were comparable to The Ground Café's. Therefore, when she described a problem with the teas or scones, he immediately chimed in with eleventh-hour solutions.

Rob phoned numerous times, and she played phone tag with him. She yearned for his quick grin, the sound of his deep voice, his warm-hearted reassurances. However, immersed in a whirlwind of activity, the hours passed all too quickly.

Another snag, Rob texted the evening after Sean's arrival. *I'm coming, but delayed a few more days. I should be in Roses by Friday.*

Understandable, she replied, noting Friday was a week away. *I'll send photos of my new menu.*

Sean watched while she texted Rob and smiled knowingly. "I'm here for you," was all he said.

The following day, Kathleen went through every nook in her teahouse for elements she might have missed. Lightly, she traced her fingers over the herbal tea baskets, honey dispensers, and a row of clear glass pitchers. Teddy's crew had completed the renovation, and the place was quiet, save for a collection of Irish tunes playing on the CD.

Everything in the teahouse was unique and stylish, a far cry from the greasy, cramped, and gloomy interior she'd first encountered. She knew Rob would be impressed.

Rob.

She'd meant to send him photos of the menu. In the flurry of activity, she'd forgotten, falling into bed at night too weary to think. She'd do it in the morning.

"What will the children drink?" Sean came up behind her and interrupted her thoughts.

"What children?"

"Your customers will bring in their wee ones. You'll want to keep them content and occupied."

"I can serve hot cocoa."

"What about a fun tea experience?" He inclined his head. "Brew decaffeinated tea and give it an unusual name—like cinnamon toast tea served in a cup named Chip."

"A chipped cup?"

"From *Beauty and the Beast*," he prompted.

"Oh, right." She smiled. "Brilliant. Let's include that name on the chalkboard."

Later the same day, a $6000 invoice arrived for the double-deck gas convection oven. It was stamped OVERDUE.

Kathleen scanned the bill and gasped.

Sean peered over her shoulder. "Troubles?"

"How can the supplier expect payment if I'm not even

open yet?" She set the invoice on the counter and began mixing dough for wheat bread. For her, baking was therapeutic and gave her something to do with her hands. "Financially, I'm stretched to the max."

"You can't apply for another loan?"

"I'm considered an upstart, and banks don't risk their money. I put up my parent's home in County Galway that was deeded to me upon their death as collateral. After $200,000 dollars, I'm tapped out."

He lifted a dark eyebrow, then perused the letter accompanying the invoice. "The company can shut you down if you can't remit."

"Naturally I pay my bills. Just not until the teahouse opens."

"I can help."

She placed the dough into the electric mixer and switched it on. "Sean, I refuse to accept your money. I know you're not a rich man."

The electricity blew out with a snap. The lights switched off, and the mixer stopped.

"Again?" she groaned. "Teddy said we may have an electrical issue if this keeps up, although the power company blames the problem on the new lines being dug in the area. I hope they're right, because I don't have an extra five thousand—"

"At present, it's an easy fix," Sean assured, finding the breaker box and switching the power back on. Once the mixer started running again, he showed up beside her.

"Kathleen, I have a business proposition for you," he said.

"I already had one."

"From your hotshot Miami boyfriend?"

She winced. She'd confided to Sean about Rob's job proposal. She wished she hadn't. A day hadn't gone by when

Sean didn't bring up Rob, and his remarks were never flattering.

"I'm not selling my teahouse and setting back to Ireland with my tail between my legs," she declared, "so don't tell me to give up."

"We Irish have more pride than that."

There it was again. *We versus them.* The Irish versus the Americans, the bankers, even Teddy's crewmen if Sean disagreed with their work. He constantly implied the Irish were underdogs and appealed to her sense of patriotism.

She shut off the mixer, wrested the dough from the bowl, and began kneading. "What are you saying?"

"We share a passion for this type of place." He sidled closer. Instinctively, she moved back a step. "You and I worked under brass-hat Brady and watched him make difficult decisions."

"So?"

"So let's face the truth. You can't run a business. You're too emotionally involved." His tone challenged with a hint of mockery. "And there are numerous details, far too many for one person. You're in over your head, luv. Hey, you can't even make a decision about curtains without help."

Luv. She let the word go by.

She kept her head down while she rolled out the dough, then dusted her flour-stained hands along the edges of her apron. "As you obviously guessed, my specialty isn't interior design."

"This isn't about decorating. This is about realizing your strengths and admitting your weaknesses."

Rather than argue, she agreed, because she knew arguing with him was useless. He was always willing to fight, and she didn't have the energy. Despite the never-ending work hours, her problems continued to mushroom. Somewhere along the way, she'd begun to feel powerless.

Maybe Sean was right. Her corporate sense wasn't strong. Sure, she'd been in positions of management, but that was different from owning a company where every choice meant financial loss and subsequent failure.

She sank onto a high-backed chair. "What are you suggesting?"

"As I said, I'm offering a firm proposition and subsequent solution."

Her eyebrows flicked upward, measuring him. "Which is?"

"I'll buy into your business." He watched her closely as he pulled up a chair. "Your financial worries will end, and you'll be free to bake and serve customers—the services you did best at The Ground Café."

"Your terms ..."

He slid his chair closer, then stretched out his legs. "A 60/40 split. In my favor."

"Absolutely not." Firmly, she shook her head. "I did all the groundwork."

"I'll continue your vision going forward, so don't go flashing those blustery eyes at me." With both hands on his knees, he leaned forward. "I'll take over all business aspects, financial and otherwise, and you can concentrate on a successful opening day."

"Sean, this is a difficult conversation." She rubbed the middle of her forehead and closed her eyes. "Give me time to consider."

"Rest assured I have your best interests at heart. In fact, I'll draw up the necessary papers." He lifted her chin. "It's best for everyone, aye?"

A heaviness invaded her body. Quieting, she gazed down at her rumpled apron, her washed-out jeans, and tried not to twist her hands. She was cornered, and her teahouse deserved no less than the best. She surveyed her supply of china cups and saucers stacked neatly on the shelves, the double-deck gas convection oven. What would happen if she lost her oven because of nonpayment? Her teahouse couldn't survive without the main oven and a large dough mixer, and she'd run out of funds.

"I'll think about it," she replied.

But what about Nancy, the new girl she'd hired, who seemed genuinely interested in learning the tea business?

Kathleen's mind whirled in a thousand different directions.

Four more days went by. Four more nights she spent staring at the ceiling in her shabby apartment, seeking the serenity of sleep before it vanished, forcing prolonged hours of insomnia and torturous deliberations.

And somewhere along the way, she stopped communicating with Rob altogether.

CHAPTER ELEVEN

On Wednesday of the following week, Rob strode over the tiny white blossoms lacing the front porch of Kathleen's teahouse. He knocked, then opened the wooden door. A tiny bell announced his arrival, though no one acknowledged him.

He'd texted his flight information to Kathleen the night before and she hadn't replied. In fact, he hadn't heard a word from her in several days. A quick query to Candee assured Kathleen was well, albeit "busy beyond words". Still, the silence had prompted him to return to Roses a couple days early.

Despite his focus on Miami and the mountain of paperwork yet to be signed, he congratulated himself. He'd successfully sold his business to a group of managers who'd worked in his bakeries for years. They'd pooled their funds, the bank loans were secured, and the closing was slated in a month.

"Sorry, fella. We're not open until St. Patrick's Day." A pencil-thin man sporting a dark beard and curly hair sat at a round table in the center of the main dining room. He was unmistakably Irish, his dialect quick, his sentences running together. He straightened from his sprawling position and refilled his glass of iced tea. "Come back Saturday for our grand opening."

"I'm aware of when March seventeenth is." Disregarding the man's hostile gaze, Rob strode further into the room.

"You Americans are smarter than people give you credit for."

"Who are you?" Rob demanded.

"Sean."

"Yeah, I figured."

"You?" came Sean's clipped inquiry.

"Rob."

"Aye. Without a doubt." Sean's derisive grin followed his flippant acknowledgement. He lifted his glass. "My only defense against the warm weather. In Ireland, March is a cold, rainy month. Here, the sun shines almost continuously and it's a bit warm for me."

"You'd melt in Miami then," Rob said. "How long have you been in Roses?"

"A few days."

Rob corralled his anger, focusing on the welcoming environment of the teahouse. The stunning renovation was a treasure trove. Orderly shelves displayed simple fruit jellies and preserves, and the counter was stocked with freshly ground coffee and an assortment of loose herbal teas in glass jars. The entire space was airy and bright. On the corner of each table, he noted a container.

Sean followed his gaze. "We added those for cell-phones. Kathleen believes in conversation with no interruptions."

Rob grimaced, recalling the number of times his chats with Kathleen had been cut off by his familiar cell-phone ping.

"Hungry?" Sean raised a silver tray laden with croissants.

"Nope." Rob avoided meeting the man's assessing stare. "Where is she?"

Sunshine eased through the floral curtains, lighting the cozy atmosphere, offset by candles shimmering along an antique sideboard. The cashmere comfort of a welcoming warmth enveloped him. In that instant, Rob saw the realization of Kathleen's remarkable achievement.

Well done, Kathleen.

"She's baking another Keiran O'Malley recipe in her apartment, because she prefers her small oven," Sean was saying. "Keiran has Irish relatives, you see."

"I'm aware."

"He's a decent bloke and has made me feel right at home. His pub is fierce and just the thing after a knackered day in a scorching kitchen."

"And I'm interested in Kathleen, not you." Rob crossed his arms. "I'll wait for her here and you can be on your way."

Since he'd entered, Rob had been struggling with an escalating annoyance, standing by while Sean lazily drank iced tea and tamped up croissant crumbs from his plate with his fingers. He felt like a panhandler waiting to be granted an audience with a queen.

"I'd suggest *you* should be the one on your way." Sean's sharp voice cut through Rob's thoughts. "You're acting like a Holy Joe coming to her rescue, but as you can see, we're ready for our opening and things have gone swimmingly. And we did it all without brainy old you."

"Excuse me?" In three strides, Rob closed the distance between them. "*We're* ready? *Our* opening? What's going on here?"

"I'll blame your questions on poor hearing because of your age and not poor listening. As you Americans speak frankly, I'll frame this so that you understand. Crack on and leave."

"Don't tell me what to do," Rob warned. "This isn't your

place." He yanked out his cell-phone and typed Kathleen a text. *Where are you? I'm standing in your dining room.*

"On the contrary, it *is* my place." Sean examined his well-manicured fingernails. "Kathleen has agreed to make me her business partner. I'm here for the long haul."

For a moment, Rob couldn't trust himself to reply, his brain registering disbelief. His narrowed gaze examined Sean's blasé expression.

"I don't believe it. Kathleen is self-reliant."

Sean shrugged. "She's going in a different direction."

"Indeed?" Rob inquired. "Tell me more."

He'd been gone only a short while and Sean had triumphantly wormed his way back into her life. Slowly, something inside Rob began to crumble. While he was working out details and selling everything for her, she was handing over her business to this pompous Irishman.

He recalled his phone call with Kathleen when she'd sprung to Sean's defense.

"*Do you remember Sean, my coworker at The Ground Café?*" she'd asked.

"*The guy who is supposedly interested in quitting his manager job in Ireland to lend you a hand in America?*"

"*I wouldn't put it that way, Rob. Sean isn't supposedly interested. He is interested and assured he won't accept a salary if he were to come here.*"

Rob scrubbed a hand over his face. He should've known Sean wouldn't waste a second quitting his job, flying over the Atlantic Ocean and coming to Kathleen's rescue. Nevertheless, she considered Sean a friend, so Rob was willing to endure the rest of the exchange for her sake.

"What are the terms of this offer?" Rob asked. "Because I can make her a better one."

"Can you? Mine is a 60/40 split."

"She'd agree to that?" Rob barked a laugh. "I'm surprised."

"We've always been brilliant together, and I'm her new fella. She's a fine thing, isn't she?"

Rob grappled with a stab of jealousy. "I can afford to give her the world," he said quietly.

"Your wealth doesn't impress me or Kathleen. How dare you flaunt your money around?" Sean enunciated each word in a vicious, thick brogue. "She's thrilled with our recent agreement."

"Oh, am I now, Sean?" Kathleen stormed into the room, her face emanating pure outrage. By the looks of the two steps she'd walked, she'd been in the doorway for some time. The green ribbon tying back her silky hair was askew, and her dark eyes sparked with fury.

Rob's heart thumped in double time, his gaze riveted on her. He trod closer, intending to take her in his embrace. She shrugged him off and marched to within a foot of Sean.

"How are ya, luv?" Sean grinned.

"Luv? Luv? I never decided on any so-called agreement."

"You were earwigging?" Sean shoved his glass aside and rose to his feet. "Eavesdropping on a private chat?"

She stamped her foot. "This is *my* teahouse, not yours."

Her outburst earned her Sean's hangdog expression. "Kathleen, I beg your forgiveness. Just teasing. Obviously, you're a bundle of nerves with St. Paddy's looming. If you'll only—"

"Get out and don't come back."

"What? And go where—" he sputtered.

"Back to Boston, or Ireland. You've ruined it for yourself by your underhandedness." She shook her head and whispered, "I should've realized. Why do I never learn?"

Without so much as picking up his glass or bidding a courteous goodbye, Sean twisted on his heels and blustered through the front door with lengthy, purposeful strides.

"A sound good riddance to him," Rob said as the door slammed. "Now you and I can talk."

Whirling, her glare blasted fury. "As if I'm starving for a chat with you when you're always so preoccupied. I don't need you, and I don't need Sean."

"We've been separated for a while, but now I'm retired. Let's sit down and have a friendly discussion over a cup of tea. Candee mentioned you received an overdue bill for the gas convection oven. I can help by writing out—"

Kathleen's eyes widened, and tears erupted. "How can you be so brilliant and yet think you can buy me? I know what I want, and I can achieve it on my own."

"But I can fix this." He paused. He loathed saying the same words his father had used on him, and it hadn't resolved anything.

Inside his jacket pocket, his cell-phone rang.

She stepped behind a high-backed chair, as if fortifying herself against him. Deliberately, she unclasped the skeleton key locket from her neck and placed it on the chair.

He felt as if his heart was breaking. He rubbed his fist against his chest. His eyes blurred with the effort.

His phone kept ringing.

"Aren't you going to answer?" she asked.

"Later." He came forward and closed his hand over her shoulder. "It's not important."

More tears leaked from her eyes and rolled down her cheeks. He brushed them away, and she flinched.

"Rob, return to Miami where you obviously belong."

They were so close he could see the mix of emotions crossing her face—trembling chin, lips pressed together, the slight freckles dotting her wet cheeks.

"You must know how much I love you," he said.

She drew an inward breath. "Everyone seems to love me

these days." Despite her quaking voice, she remained perfectly still.

"I realize you're joking. I know how you Irish love to—"

"This Irishwoman is deadly serious." Her voice rose. "And another thing, which I'm certain will come as a shocking surprise to you: this business is mine, and mine alone."

CHAPTER TWELVE

At noon a day later, Kathleen sat in a high-backed chair in her teahouse and went through her text messages. Rob hadn't returned since their argument.

Instead, he'd called and left messages, saying he was staying at Candee and Teddy's home if she needed him.

Here's a final idea, he'd texted. *I've partnered with the Roses Chamber of Commerce for a ribbon-cutting ceremony on your official opening day. I know it's late but every bit of advertising helps.*

She hadn't responded.

I've done more market research and can set up a paid advertising media blitz which will coincide with St. Patrick's Day.

No. She'd set up all her online advertising ahead of time. She didn't need to lean on anyone except herself.

Why won't you let me help you? he'd asked again and again. *If you give us half a chance, you will remember how good we r together.*

That dart effectively pierced a nerve, and she'd closed her cell-phone and placed it in her purse.

A soft opening at the teahouse was arranged to begin at four o'clock. This gave her and Nancy, the new employee, a chance to work out the crimps. Although the public was aware the teahouse was launching, Kathleen hadn't actively publicized it. Candee and Teddy sent their regards, as Joseph was participating in a horse show in Asheville and they couldn't attend. Keiran and Desiree were swamped at O'Malley's. And Sean had fled Roses.

Fortunately, another power outage hadn't occurred while customers dined later that evening, although the lock on the women's bathroom door broke.

Kathleen had also teamed up with Keiran and chalked his mushroom stroganoff as a main dinner entrée, quickly learning that serving the dish at five o'clock was too early and nine too late. Patrons preferred their dinner hour at seven, and she'd soon run out of mushroom stroganoff.

By nine p.m., the teahouse had emptied. After Nancy helped clean, she'd scanned a text message on her phone and departed without an explanation, forgetting her house keys in her haste. Because Nancy lived with her parents on the outskirts of Roses, Kathleen assumed she wouldn't need the keys until morning. Just in case, she put them aside near the herbal tea jars.

Kathleen dreaded the silence that enveloped the unoccupied rooms. It allowed her mind to dwell on all she'd lost. No longer could she hide behind work and busyness. She was forced to confront how much she missed Rob.

She slumped in the loveseat near the foyer and picked up her phone. She planned to make notes about the soft opening, tweaking her original vision. Despite her attempts, she couldn't focus, too intent on the honorable, caring man who had stolen her heart.

He'd been justifiably hurt and angry when he'd returned from Miami to find Sean lounging in her teahouse. And jealous, hiding his emotions by offering her money, hoping it would smooth the rift between them.

Her heart pinched. He'd worked for years to ensure a

prosperous business, and desperately wanted her to succeed as well. He was the type of guy who helped people, soft-hearted and obliging. She knew he would never refuse her any favor. Rob was a man she could always count on.

He loved her. He'd told her so.

And what had she done when he'd proclaimed his love?

Why, she'd thrown it in his face.

"You must know how much I love you," he'd said.

"Everyone seems to love me these days," she'd responded coolly.

She read his numerous texts, pleading with her to give them a second chance.

She hadn't replied.

He had inquired about attending her soft opening.

I'd prefer you didn't. Please take my advice and stay in Miami.

And then he'd gone dark and hadn't contacted her since.

Dejectedly, she put her head in her hands and sobbed. Somehow, she'd done it again—succeeded in being involved in a heartbreaking romance with a man.

No. That wasn't true. Rob had given up his life in Miami, his thriving career, *everything* for her. And in the shared hours exploring a ghost town and dancing Irish jigs, amidst toppled tea cups and spilled vases filled with water and flowers, she'd fallen in love with him too.

Restless, she wiped her eyes, stood, and wandered through the vacant, lonely rooms, lighting night light candles and watering the potted green ferns.

Nothing was the same without him. The teahouse wasn't alive. He'd brought laughter, full of ideas, a ready smile on his face. And now he was gone.

She had driven him away, flatly refusing his help. She'd seen the raw sadness in his blue eyes, the sagging around his mouth, when he'd said goodbye and walked out the door.

She leaned a shoulder on the windowpane and stared out at a cloudless night. Somewhere in the distance, a church bell pealed. When the time neared midnight, she sighted the star-shaped Big Dipper above the northern horizon.

Half-heartedly, she murmured, "Rob, how can you be so quiet after I told you to return to Miami? Did you forget me already?"

With a tattered sigh, she retreated to the back room and burrowed through the chest of drawers. She extracted the skeleton key locket and glided her fingers over the elaborate floral design. He'd confessed she held the key to his heart and requested she wear it always.

"Rainbows are brilliant in America too, Kathleen. And Roses is your new home."

And then the words that had dangled between them.

Here. With me.

She secured the locket, feeling better when it was near her heart, where it belonged.

With trembling hands, she texted him. If he accepted her apology and boarded a plane from Miami in the morning, he might arrive in Roses by midday. There was so much she needed to tell him. She'd been hurt by men countless times in her life and had been afraid to trust again. To love again.

But what was the world without love?

A few minutes after midnight brought a ping to Rob's cell-phone. He'd been sitting by the guest bedroom's window in Candee's home, gazing idly outside at the familiar Big Dipper. The house was quiet, as the family was attending a horse show in Asheville.

"It better not be another manager texting me at this hour," he muttered, yanking the phone from his pocket.

Kathleen's caller ID appeared on the screen.

I miss you. Would you consider flying back from Miami?

And then: *1-800-IRELAND.*

He couldn't contain his excitement. He was already on his feet, his heart pounding with joy.

The drive to Kathleen's teahouse, which normally took under ten minutes, he covered in less than five. He didn't know what he'd say, wasn't sure how she'd respond. All that mattered was she had reached out to him and he was able to see her again.

He knocked once, hesitating only a second outside the teahouse's door, feeling the cool nip in the night air against his heated cheeks. Realizing the door was unlocked, he stepped inside. The tinkling bell announced his arrival.

She sat on a velvet loveseat in the foyer, her back to him, peering at a lengthy list. He recognized the business plan they'd drawn up together.

"Nancy?" Kathleen inquired without glancing up. "I put your keys aside for you. You'll see them by the tea jars on the counter."

He longed to rush to her, to pull her into his arms. She looked vulnerable, her red-gold hair shining in the delicate candlelight. Twice, he'd left her alone when he'd flown to Miami.

"Kathleen," he said.

She twisted and flew to her feet. "Rob?" All color drained from her complexion. "You're here? How?"

"I never left Roses."

"I thought you were in Miami."

"I couldn't leave." He strode to a cell-phone container and slipped his phone inside. "Our life together wasn't finished. It hadn't even started."

She moistened her lips, raced to him, and looped her arms around his neck.

He cradled her and guided her to the loveseat. She wore his locket over a starched white shirt and tailored black pants —the uniform she'd decided on for the teahouse. He traced his fingers along her high cheekbones. Her long dark lashes fluttered.

"I wish you'd been here, for the soft opening," she said.

"I wanted to. I'm here now. How did it go?"

"A few tweaks. Actually more than a few." She snuggled nearer his chest. "I learned people in Roses like to eat dinner at seven o'clock and be home early. The place cleared out by nine."

His lips brushed her forehead. "That's what a little bird told me."

She gazed up at him, this beauty he'd almost lost. "Who?" she asked.

"Nancy."

"My new employee?"

"Lovely woman, and absolutely exceptional. Sorry she'll no longer be working for you."

Rapidly, Kathleen blinked. "Excuse me?"

"Nancy will be working for me. Or rather, for us."

"You can't just walk in and steal my best employee."

"*Our* best employee."

"I'm not following." She frowned, her voice uncertain. "I finally ..."

He pressed a finger to her mouth. "I bought another place. A ghost town, actually."

"You bought ..." Incredulous, she stared at him. "You bought Hollan Farms? Now you'll be busier than ever."

"I didn't buy the town for me." He kissed her lips, softly, sweetly. "I bought the town for David to manage. I'm a silent investor."

She grinned, her face lighting with laughter. "The cow guy?"

"The one and only. And Nancy will help him." Rob twirled a lock of Kathleen's silky hair around his fingers. "Those two are young and ambitious. Hey, maybe it's the start of a budding romance. And you and I can oversee their progress once in a while."

"What will you do in the meantime?" she asked.

"I'm retired." He grinned. "But I'll be around, just in case you need my assistance."

"I do." She sat straighter, meeting his gaze with her own. "And I finally realized that accepting help isn't a sign of weakness, but of strength."

"You'll be far more able to reach your goals."

"Aye. So I've learned."

"Since you're so agreeable," he stood, then got down on one knee. "Will you marry an American man like me?"

"This is really happening," she murmured. "And my answer is, aye. Yes."

His smile reached his ears, and he went back to cuddling her on the loveseat. "After St. Patrick's Day, we'll look for a home in Roses," he said.

"I like the mild weather here. In Ireland, the days get dark quickly in the winter, and it's rainy and cold."

"In Miami, it's too hot most of the year."

Her deep brown eyes brimmed with tears. "Then Roses is perfect." She snuggled into his arms as his lips moved over hers.

"I love you more than anyone in the world," he whispered. "When you told me to leave, I vowed to wait however long it might take. I knew we had something extraordinary together."

"I've always wanted to visit Miami."

"I've always wanted to visit Ireland. I even have their toll-free number."

She laughed. "You don't really think that if you punch in 1-800-IRELAND, someone from Ireland will answer?"

With aching tenderness, he said, "I believe she will."

"I love you," she whispered.

"And I love you."

In the container by a table, his cell-phone rang.

She grinned up at him. "Ireland calling?"

"Toll-free."

"Aren't you going to answer it?"

"Nope. She's already answered all my dreams." He gazed around her comfortable teahouse, then at the exquisite woman in his arms.

A forever love.

THE END

RECIPE FOR AUNTIE PEGGY'S IRISH BROWN BREAD

6 cups seedless raisins

2 cups raisin water. Save after cooking the raisins

Cover the raisins with water. Cook until tender. Drain but SAVE two cups of the liquid after cooking.

DRY

7 cups sifted, all-purpose flour

1 teaspoon allspice

4 teaspoons cinnamon

2 teaspoons nutmeg

4 teaspoons baking soda

WET

1 cup butter, softened/room temperature

3 cups sugar. Quantity is adjustable

6 large eggs, room temperature.

If you wish, set aside the raisin water that is left and freeze it. Use it the next time you cook the raisins. Then, reduce the sugar by a cup. If using fewer than six cups of raisins to start with, reduce the sugar.

All ingredients should be at room temperature.

Sift together all the dry ingredients in a large bowl and set aside.

Blend the butter, sugar and eggs. (I like to use the KitchenAid mixer for this step.)

Add the 2 cups of raisin liquid to the wet ingredients and mix well.

Add the wet mixture to the dry mix.

Stir in the 6 cups of cooked raisins and blend well.

Pour into four greased loaf pans. Bake for 1 to 1.25 hours at 325 degrees.

The top will spring back when touched lightly or a toothpick/cake tester works.

A NOTE FROM JOSIE

Dear Friend,

Thank you for reading *1-800-IRELAND.* I hope you enjoyed it. This the third book in my contemporary sweet romance series: *Flipping for You.*

In this story, the 1-800 series continues in the charming town of Roses, North Carolina, and follows 1-800-CUPID, and 1-800-CHRISTMAS.

In 1-800-IRELAND, I gave Kathleen, from Oh Danny Boy, her own story. And, because Rob is a reader favorite from previous 1-800 books, I decided to give him his own book.

Then, take a beach trip with Belle and Andrew to beautiful Wilmington and read 1-800-SUMMER.

If you loved this sweet romance as much as I loved writing it, please help other people find *1-800-IRELAND* by posting your amazing review here, as well as for the bundle: Irish Hearts

1-800-IRELAND is available in ebook, paperback, Large Print paperback, and audiobook.

I'd love to meet you in person someday, but in the meantime, all I can offer is a sincere and grateful thank you. Without your support, my books would not be possible.

As I write my next sweet or inspirational romance, remember this: Have you ever tried something you were afraid to try because it mattered so much to you? I did, when I started writing. Take the chance, and just do something you love.

My Spotify Play List for 1-800-IRELAND is here.

With sincere appreciation,

Josie Riviera

Want more sweet Irish romances?

Oh Danny Boy: A reader favorite! This pot of gold could hold more than they bargained for...

Maeve: Set on the exotic island of Corsica, France.

He's all business. She loves to laugh. When business conflicts with pleasure, what could possibly go wrong?

A Chocolate-Box Irish Wedding:

A woman who wanted more. A man who wanted her. Can they rediscover their love in the seaside town where it all began?

Irish Hearts:

All 4 book in 1 collection!

ACKNOWLEDGMENTS

An appreciative thank you to my patient husband, Dave, and our three wonderful children.

ABOUT THE AUTHOR

Josie Riviera is a *USA TODAY* bestselling author of contemporary, inspirational, and historical sweet romances that read like Hallmark movies. She lives in the Charlotte, NC, area with her wonderfully supportive husband. They share their home with an adorable shih tzu, who constantly needs grooming, and live in an old house forever needing renovations.

Become a member of my Read and Review VIP Facebook group for exclusive giveaways and ARCs.

To connect with Josie, visit her webpage and subscribe to her newsletter. As a thank-you, she'll send you a free sweet romance novella directly to your inbox.

josieriviera.com

ALSO BY JOSIE RIVIERA

Seeking Patience

Seeking Catherine (always Free!)

Seeking Fortune

Seeking Charity

Seeking Rachel

The Seeking Series

Oh Danny Boy

I Love You More

A Snowy White Christmas

A Portuguese Christmas

Holiday Hearts Book Bundle Volume One

Holiday Hearts Book Bundle Volume Two

Holiday Hearts Book Bundle Volume Three

Holiday Hearts Volume Four

Candleglow and Mistletoe

Maeve (Perfect Match)

A Christmas To Cherish

A Love Song To Cherish

A Valentine To Cherish

A Christmas Puppy To Cherish

Romance Stories To Cherish

Aloha to Love

Sweet Peppermint Kisses

Valentine Hearts Boxed Set

1-800-CUPID

1-800-CHRISTMAS

1-800-IRELAND

1-800-SUMMER

The 1-800-Series Sweet Contemporary Romance Bundle

Irish Hearts Sweet Romance Bundle

Holly's Gift

A Chocolate-Box Valentine

A Chocolate-Box Christmas

A Chocolate-Box New Years

A Chocolate-Box Summer Breeze

A Chocolate-Box Christmas Wish

A Chocolate-Box Irish Wedding

Chocolate-Box Hearts

Chocolate-Box Hearts Volume Two

Recipes from the Heart

Leading Hearts

MAEVE (A SWEET CONTEMPORARY ROMANCE) PREVIEW

"It'll do you good to get away from Ireland. We've had a rainy summer."

"Rainy summer?" Maeve Doherty grinned at her best

friend, Colleen O'Keefe, who was busily swiping Maeve's phone. "When can you recall a non-wet summer in Ireland?"

"A year ago. It was on a Thursday."

Maeve laughed out loud. As always, her flaming-haired friend's sunny disposition lifted her spirits.

Colleen chuckled in return. Her tailored canary-yellow pantsuit, with matching pumps, fit her full-figured body impeccably. Maeve glanced at her own worn linen skirt and smoothed her wrinkled polyester blouse. When had she last taken time for herself? She'd forgotten, it had been so long ago, with all the worry and sleepless nights.

Colleen plunked into an oversized chair in the lobby of the building that housed the Merrimac Company. The women were purchasing agents for a small Irish hotel chain. Their duties included placing orders for everything from hotel furniture to cleaning supplies, and comparing various prices and the quality of the merchandise.

Colleen pointed with one of her French manicured fingernails at Maeve's phone screen. "If I'm reading this email correctly, you've been offered a free week at the paradise island of your choice, compliments of the Perfect Match dating agency."

Maeve pulled up a chair across from her friend. "Aye."

Keeping her fingertip on the blinking cursor, Colleen paused. "You plan to accept, don't you?"

"Whatever the catch is, it's not worth a week anywhere on the globe."

"This offer is from Amy Yates, your friend from America, and her husband, Dawson. And it's a personalized invitation." Colleen scanned Maeve's phone screen. "A free vacation, a romantic getaway, a chance—"

Maeve held up a hand. "Aye."

"So it's legit," Colleen declared gaily. "I remember you said they owned the agency."

"Aye."

"Which island are you choosing?"

"I'm not choosing any island because I'm not going."

"How about Corsica, France?" Colleen obviously pretended she hadn't heard Maeve. "You've always wanted to learn French. And isn't there a famous museum there you've always wanted to visit?"

"Maison Bonaparte, the ancestral home of the Bonaparte family." Maeve nodded. "The museum is located in Ajaccio, Corsica."

"Then go."

"Yes, someday, on my own, using my own money—not obligated to a matchmaking agency."

Colleen pushed her glasses up her nose and peered at the phone. "All expenses are paid and the terms and conditions are clearly spelled out. All you have to do is agree to spend the week with your match or risk being charged for the vacation."

Maeve lifted a skeptical eyebrow. "That's all?"

"It's a massive marketing campaign to introduce their new business," Colleen reminded her. "You're helping them as much as they're helping you."

"I love history, but I'm not that desperate to see Napoléon Bonaparte's death mask. I'd prefer spending a cozy week in my flat reading a pile of European history books." Maeve tapped her fingers together and drew in a breath. "Figure in a hot cuppa Irish tea and lemon scones from The Ground Café and I'll be merry as a leprechaun."

"You're emotionally spent," her friend said quietly. "And you gave Amy Yates permission to plug your name into the Perfect Match database."

Maeve turned a despairing look on Colleen. "Aye, in a flash of desperation when I feared any opportunity for love was passing me by. I'm over that."

Was she?

Once she'd recovered from the sadness and shock of learning her twenty-year-old brother Owen had been diagnosed with cancer, she'd settled into the daily task of tending to him when he opted to move in with her rather than live with their mother. She'd given up every pastime she enjoyed to care for him, including auditioning for minor acting roles, something she loved.

Now that Owen's radiation treatments were over and his caregiving routine had become stable, perhaps she could ease up a bit, take a breather. Perhaps ...

"Maeve?" Colleen prodded. "Owen is in remission and he can go live with your mother for a week. She's able-bodied and can tend to him. You're only twenty-six. Live your life."

"Most days my mother isn't capable of washing a dish, let alone attending to a sick adult. She had a hard-enough time being a parent when Owen was well."

"Your mother lands in the middle of drama because of the type of men she sees, and her ongoing dilemmas can't always be your problem." Colleen leaned back in her chair. Her normally keen bright-blue gaze softened. "Enough about your mother. What's the craic with you? Are you sleeping okay?"

Maeve shrugged. "I'm always tired, although everyone is exhausted nowadays because of our hectic lifestyles."

"Grab this chance. Go. Believe me, if it weren't for my boyfriend, Colin, I'd take your place."

Colleen and Colin had an on-again, off-again relationship that had lasted for over a year. Currently, it was on again.

A reassuring grin crossed Colleen's freckled face. "Along with Owen's healthcare providers, your mother will mind him brilliantly. I want to see an optimistic smile on your face again. I'm sure you'll have a lorry-load of stories to share when you get back."

Maeve shook her head. "Because of all the days I missed

when Owen became ill, I'm on the verge of losing my job. I certainly can't afford to take off any more time. Besides, his medical bills are mounting, and our private insurance only covers part of them."

"You're physically and mentally exhausted. *Your* health is important too. You need the time away to maintain your sense of balance."

"Aye, perhaps," Maeve admitted. Her brother's cancer journey had been a lengthy road crowded with difficult decisions and the challenges of radiation treatment.

"The Merrimac Company wants to branch out of Ireland and explore resort areas for other hotels. Pitch the idea to our manager. Tell Mrs. McShea it's a working holiday. Just think you'll get paid for sitting on a beach in a bikini."

"I don't swim, and I've never worn a bikini."

"Live a wee bit, Maeve. Spend your days lying in a lounge chair and looking out at the Mediterranean. You once told me there are over two hundred beaches in Corsica. Imagine the sun, the surf—"

"Colleen—"

"The sand." Colleen laughed. "It's a win-win. Besides, who can pass up the chance to meet Mr. Right?"

"I'm too busy to fritter away my valuable time on a man. And there's no such man as Mr. Right, at least not for me."

"How do you know? Make the time."

"Suppose he's not interesting?"

"Suppose he is?"

"What about Crinkles?"

"Your dog is accustomed to your ma's flat." Colleen tapped the phone screen again. Amy says her agency's matchmaking algorithms are the best and they're launching this campaign to prove it."

"And if you keep scrolling, you'll see they want people who've been unlucky in love."

Like her.

Maeve studied Merrimac's lobby—a gleaming brown floor, mahogany table, anything but her friend's sympathetic stare. She'd spilled out more than she'd intended.

A year ago while visiting a cousin in America, she'd met Amy while shopping in an exclusive boutique, not realizing at first that she was chatting with the owner of the boutique. They'd become instant friends, and they shared coffee and heartfelt conversation after the store closed. That evening, Maeve had poured out her sadness to her new-found confidante.

Finbar, Maeve's boyfriend of two years, had broken up with her—not even in person—but through a dismissive text.

"No more," she'd declared to Amy. "Men and their hollow promises are not to be believed."

Wasn't Maeve's father, who'd left her mother without an explanation, further proof of her statement? He'd said he'd return. He never had.

"Maeve? Maeve?" Colleen yanked Maeve from her upsetting remembrances. "I'm partial to the final line of your dating profile." She read aloud: "'Love comes in many forms, and I believe in a commitment to one person.' Colleen looked up at Maeve. "Aww, that's very sweet. You expressed yourself perfectly."

Heat rose in Maeve's face. "I'm starry-eyed and foolish for writing something so reckless. No one stays with one person forever."

"Some do. Some people have a love that lasts. Where are those rose-colored glasses you used to wear?"

"I've put them away and become realistic."

"Dust them off. What if Mr. Right is waiting for you in Corsica?"

"He won't be, although just to be sure ..." Maeve grabbed

her phone from Colleen and included another line at the bottom of her dating profile.

Be warned ... I'm a workaholic.

Colleen squinted at the screen. "Being a workaholic is supposed to deter him?"

"I'll plead nine-to-five obligations."

Plus, any other excuses necessary to safeguard her heart.

"So, it's settled." Colleen flashed a quick smile. "You'll accept Amy's offer and choose Corsica."

"Aye." Maeve feigned enthusiasm, then blew out a breath.

She'd go, she'd rest, she'd work. But she wouldn't risk falling in love.

Once was enough. Besides, if there was a perfect match for her on God's emerald-green planet, she'd have found him by now in Ireland.

"That's grand," Colleen said. "Finally, you're doing something for yourself." With a flourish, Colleen stood and walked over to Maeve, throwing her arms around her. "Get ready, my dear friend, for an amazing adventure!"

***** End of excerpt *Maeve* by Josie Riviera**

***

Want more? Keep reading Maeve on Amazon.

Free on Kindle Unlimited!

Made in the USA
Coppell, TX
21 March 2021

52105329R00094